DRAWING

A JAKE MORGAN MYSTERY

DEAD

DRAWING

A JAKE MORGAN MYSTERY

DEAD

Rick Gadziola

ECW Press

Copyright © Rick Gadziola, 2006

Published by ECW PRESS
2120 Queen Street East, Suite 200, Toronto, Ontario, Canada M4E 1E2

All rights reserved. No part of this publication may be reproduced, stored in a retrieval system, or transmitted in any form by any process — electronic, mechanical, photocopying, recording, or otherwise — without the prior written permission of the copyright owners and ECW PRESS.

NATIONAL LIBRARY OF CANADA CATALOGUING IN PUBLICATION

Gadziola, Rick
Drawing dead : Rick Gadziola.

(A Jake Morgan mystery)
ISBN 10: 1-55022-738-6
ISBN 13: 978-1-55022-738-3

I. Title. II. Series: Gadziola, Rick. Jake Morgan mystery.

PS8613.A398D73 2006   C813'.6   C2006-904116-4

Editor: Michael Holmes
Cover and Text Design: Tania Craan
Production & Typesetting: Mary Bowness
Printing: Transcontinental

This book is set in Serif and Minion.

The publication of *Drawing Dead* has been generously supported by the Canada Council, the Ontario Arts Council, the Ontario Media Development Corporation, and the Government of Canada through the Book Publishing Industry Development Program. Canadä

DISTRIBUTION
CANADA: Jaguar Book Group, 100 Armstrong Avenue, Georgetown, ON, L7G 5S4
UNITED STATES: Independent Publishers Group, 814 North Franklin Street, Chicago, Illinois 60610

PRINTED AND BOUND IN CANADA

ECW PRESS
ecwpress.com

For Susan, Paul, and Marie.

Part of the $10 million I spent on gambling, part on booze, and part on women . . . the rest I spent foolishly.
— George Raft

Chapter ♠

"She's definitely got the hots for you, Jake."

I was dealing a lively $50–$100 Pot Limit Hold 'Em game in the posh Oasis poker room. It was the Thursday before Memorial Day weekend in Las Vegas, the place was packed, and hundred-dollar bills were flying around the casino like November leaves in a New England windstorm.

The "she" being referred to was an absolutely gorgeous, middle-aged, Japanese woman who had just excused herself to visit the powder room. She had slipped me a black hundred-dollar chip, smiled suggestively, and told me to keep her seat warm and lucky, further adding to the playful innuendos with which she had been plying me for the past half-hour. Some of the males at the table believed she meant her chair, but the consensus thought otherwise.

I knew her only as "Mrs. K.," the wife of "Mr. K.," the billionaire shipping magnate and one of Vegas' top-10 "whales" who came to donate two or three times a year. She wasn't as big a contributor to the local economy as her husband, but she could still go through a million in chips faster than I could go through a bag of Lay's All Dressed.

"Ah, you guys don't know what you're talking about," I told them. "Mrs. K. is married to one of the 50 richest men in the world. I'm down to peanut butter and jelly back home and payday's still a week away."

"Not after what she's been toking you tonight," said JB, one of the young, local pros. "Look at your pocket."

"Yeah," said one of the other players, known as Stinky. "You could be havin' Special K for dinner instead, if you know what I mean."

A few of the guys laughed lewdly and gave each other the nudge-nudge, wink-wink.

"I know you're tryin' to hide it, Jake," said JB, "but you've made enough in tips tonight to get into this game yourself."

"And wouldn't I welcome that," I smiled and said, meaning it.

I finished shuffling the cards and began to deal. As I waited for the first player to make his decision of coming in or not, I glanced over to the supervisor's desk. Mrs. K. was talking to McClusky, my floor person, and the two of them were looking directly at my table.

McClusky was a throwback to the old days of Vegas and knew how to keep the customers happy. He and I had always got along, but that might have been because I was one of his top dealers at the Oasis and had been for almost three years. I'd also helped his immediate boss, Julius Contini, keep the image of the Oasis Hotel and Casino clean through some ugly incidents during the past year. McClusky listened to what Mrs. K. was saying, then he nodded his thick, square head and shook her tiny hand with one of his meaty ham hocks.

A few minutes later, McClusky arrived at my table with a couple of empty plastic chip trays and another dealer.

"Rack up Mrs. K.'s chips, Morgan," McClusky grumbled. "New dealer comin' in, gentlemen."

"Oh, oh, somebody's in trouble," said Stinky.

"What's up?" I asked. "My shift isn't —"

"Don't argue," McClusky said. "There should be $5,100 there. Mrs. K. said to leave a hundred for the chip runner when she comes by. Bring the rest to my office." He did a 180 as gracefully as a guy in a size 56 jacket could do, and trudged off with the weight of the world on his wide shoulders.

I began separating, stacking, and counting the lady's chips, wondering what the hell I was being called up on the carpet for. Despite the nice little cash-out I'd have for the night, I couldn't afford to be docked time or lose this gig. After all, there were loan sharks with spoiled kids in private schools depending on me.

"She's probably just not feeling well," JB said, noticing my concern.

Stinky snorted. "Maybe she's gonna claim sexual harassment or somethin'."

"Don't be such a horse's ass. Jake didn't do anything wrong."

I finished racking up, placed an empty tray upside down over hers, and said thank you to the players; then I walked down the corridor toward the office like a schoolboy on his way to see the principal.

"She wants what?"

"I just told ya," McClusky explained. "Take the chips up to her suite. Spend a little time with her. Have a drink. Be nice."

"What about her husband?"

"He's back in Tokyo or someplace. She's flying solo and wants to have a good time."

"But what if Mr. K. found out? You don't want to lose the guy. He's a whale."

"Not so much the last year or so. He's been spreading it around more than we like to see. Anyway, she's the one who prefers to stay and play here. Maybe next time he'll spend more time here keepin' an eye on her. Besides, I get the feelin' there might be a little *problemo* in the old matrimonial department."

"I don't know about this. . . ."

McClusky pulled back his left jacket sleeve and looked at his watch.

"It's almost ten. Socialize with her for an hour or so. I'll put you on triple-time all the way through to eight in the morning. What's the big deal? It happens all the time. We gotta take care of the high rollers."

Now it started to sink in. "Jesus Christ! Are you saying . . . you mean you want me to . . . son of a bitch, you want me to be a gigolo? Hold the phone. That's not in my job description!"

McClusky punched something into his electronic organizer, then he glanced up at me and raised a bushy eyebrow. "Don't go turnin' gay on me, okay, Jake? I remember that showgirl broad you were bangin' last year. Man, was she built," he reminisced. "What the hell was her name again?"

"Rachel," I told him, exasperated. "And I'm *not* turning gay. I'm just saying. . . ."

Damn. Why did he have to bring Rachel up? It had been almost a year and I'd just recently gotten over her. The worst part was, she was the last one I had been intimate with, and the absence of a warm and willing female body had already started to drive me up the wall.

"You're just sayin' you don't want to spend a little time with a sexy, wealthy woman who's got the hots for you and wants to get to know you better. I'm startin' to worry about you. You know, Siegfried's looking for a new partner."

"That's not what I meant. But what about the escorts the casino keeps for times like this? There must be at least ten boy toys you can call in from the bench to pinch-hit. What about Raoul, that good-looking kid from the Dominican who just started?"

McClusky shook his head. "He's tied up with some movie star tonight. Some guy who was up for Best Supporting Actor this past year."

"Actor? As in *male* actor?"

"Yup. Apparently Raoul's a switch hitter."

"Great."

"It don't matter anyway. Mrs. K. specifically asked for you. I don't know what you're so worried about; she didn't say anything about sleeping with her. Maybe she just doesn't want to go out by herself."

"But why me? I don't get it."

McClusky shook his head. "Who knows what goes on in the minds of women nowadays? I gave up tryin' to figure 'em out a long time ago. Now when the old lady goes on and on, I just listen and nod and sing 'MacArthur Park' in my head till she leaves the room."

I stood there for a moment and tried to assimilate the situation. I'm not a prude by any means, nor am I against getting together with a beautiful woman for friendly fun and frolicking. But I like to be the one in charge. The way this scenario was unfolding reeked of me being treated like a piece of meat at an auction. Admittedly, a small part of me was flattered, but that was the part that was always getting me in trouble.

"I don't know. . . ."

McClusky tapped the eraser end of a pencil against his computer keyboard. "You know, Morgan, Mr. Contini would be very disappointed if a high-profile client like Mrs. K. was made to feel unwelcome here at the Oasis by one of his employees . . . especially such a highly regarded employee like yourself."

"Ah, man, don't bring up Big Julie . . . please. Whenever he asks me for a favor I end up getting shot, drowned, punched, and kicked. Every time I help him out I wake up in some hospital room suffering from broken bones or a concussion."

"True. But don't forget what he's done for you, too. He paid all the legal fees for your girlfriend Rachel when she was in jail, paid all your hospital bills every time you did fall on your ass and hurt yourself, and even took care of your apartment being redone when those two bozos shot your place up last fall. Hell, Mr. Contini even gave you a suite at the

Oasis for the month while the work was being done."

"Jesus. . . ." Julius Contini was the owner of the Oasis Hotel and Casino. He, too, was a bit of a throwback to the old days, but he wasn't a bad guy and he was a real straight shooter. A no-bullshit kind of guy. And McClusky was right. As much as I may have done for him, he had done back for me. This little assignment couldn't end up all that terrible no matter how badly I screwed it up. Outside of having too much to drink, not being able to perform, and maybe waking up with a wicked hangover, how bad could it be? I just didn't like not being in control.

"Okay. What room?"

"Atta boy, Jake. Suite 2221. Take one for the team!"

"Yeah, right."

"Come to think of it, take the rack of chips to the cashier's cage and get an orange one. I don't want you walkin' around with all those chips. Some old lady on her way to Bingo might see you in the hallway and roll ya."

"Very funny."

"And speakin' of the cage, when you get the $5,000 chip, register it under my name, put it right in your pocket, and give it to Mrs. K. as soon as you get there. *Capice?*"

"Yeah, yeah." The truth be known, I could sometimes have a problem walking through a casino with five thou in my pocket. It was like the tables were crying out to me.

"And don't get any funny ideas, Morgan. I know the way you are. I'm going to have Security watch you on camera all the way from here to the elevator. Don't even look at a gaming table on the way. This is business."

"Yeah, some business," I told him as I made my way to the door and opened it. "I feel like some kind of *ho*."

"Hey, I know what you mean," laughed McClusky. "Vegas makes *ho*s of us all sooner or later."

"Ah, Mr. Morgan."

She was still wearing the stunning summer dress she'd had on down in the poker room, but her hair was freshly brushed and the air around her carried an intoxicating bouquet. The sounds of light riffs of jazz came from somewhere deep in the suite. Dim lights and candlelight were the choice of the evening.

"Uh, my boss asked me to bring you your money."

I dug into my pocket, proud that I hadn't spent her token, and handed the $5,000 chip to her. She took it and smiled. It was one of the most beautiful smiles I'd ever seen in my life. Not a great big, beaming, open-mouth number, but one where the corners of freshly glossed lips turned up ever so slightly, causing two sexy little dimples to send a shiver down my spine and elsewhere.

"Thank you. Won't you come in, Mr. Morgan?" She stepped back to allow me entry.

"Only if you call me Jake," I told her. I walked inside and took a deep breath to calm my nerves. "That's a wonderful perfume you're wearing."

"Thank you," she replied, as we entered the formal living room. "It's my favorite. A creation from back home called Sakiwai: a blend of rose, lily of the valley, jasmine, and lilac. I'm glad you like it."

Mrs. K. had one of the most prestigious suites the Oasis had to offer — not as large as some, but probably at least 1,500 square feet. It was done up in Americana, with a touch of Shaker, lots of hardwood, and deep pile carpets. A small library and dining room were off to the left, and I guessed the bedroom was to the right behind two closed French doors. A balcony that stretched the width of the room offered a view of The Strip, and part of the sheer curtains blew gently outside through the open sliding glass doors.

"Very nice," I said, struggling for something to say.

"It's Early American," she said. "I can't get enough of it. So different from back home."

"My condo is Middle Bachelorhood."

"Really? I'd love to see it. Have a seat, Jake. Can I get you something to drink?" She made her way to a bar built into a Hoosier cabinet.

"Yeah, sure. Whatever you're having."

What she was having turned out to be Scotch. And even through the thick crystal of the glass and the ice cubes, I could tell it had to be at least a triple. I went to sit in a leather wingback chair, but she directed me to a seat beside her on the sofa. We clinked glasses, smiled at each other, and drank.

And drank and drank and drank. We discovered we were both going to hit the big 4-oh this year, and after some small talk about where we each grew up, went to school, and our early dating experiences, the conversation swung around to her absent husband. I noticed when she handed me the last drink that she wasn't wearing any wedding rings. I also noticed she had ten to fifteen fingers on her left hand. As I struggled to grasp the rotating glass, I gave my head a shake as I tried to reduce the effects of the whiskey.

She told me that the two of them had fallen out of love years ago, yet his passion for his businesses seemed to have escalated. She said she had kept count of the days he was away and those when he was home. A year later, when the first exceeded the latter, she told her husband she wanted a divorce. He was furious and told her that she was his wife and should know her place. That was four months ago. Now she was in Vegas trying to get her head together and talk to an American lawyer who assisted their legal firm back in Tokyo. She was meeting him here at the hotel in two days.

We were on our fourth round when she asked me if I would stay for dinner.

I was feeling no pain. "Uh, yeah, sure," I stammered. "Why not?"

She laughed at my hesitancy and sat there for a moment and we looked into each other's eyes. I saw a world of loneliness and sorrow in hers, and I wanted to reach out. I couldn't imagine what she saw in mine, except for some bloodshot veins that might be coming on. She brought out that special little smile again, leaned over, and gave me a soft kiss that lingered for just a second or two.

"Yes, by all means," I said with authority. "I will stay for dinner, Mrs. K."

"If I am to call you Jake, then you will call me Kyoko."

The next kiss lingered twice as long, and as our mouths were about to part, she broke the contact. She was trembling ever so slightly and her eyes became moist.

"Perhaps we could discuss dessert over dinner," she finally said with a laugh.

I gave her my answer with the biggest grin I'd had in months. "Definitely."

"Well, if you can amuse yourself for 15 minutes, I spent most of the day shopping and I would really love to have a quick bath. If you don't mind?"

"Only if you promise to put more of that Suzuki on."

"That's *Sakiwai*, silly," she said. "And I'll be sure to put it on." She smiled seductively. "Everywhere."

"Mmm. I'll drink to that."

She found that funny and laughed. "We'll order room service when I get out."

"Sounds good," I said, feeling tipsy but becoming more confident in the situation. "I'm all yours."

She had reached the French doors, opened them, and stepped inside. As she closed the doors she called out, "And I'll drink to that."

◆

I fiddled around with the plasma-screen television to check on the baseball games I had bet a few bucks on. I had won two of the early games and the last one was in extra innings. This would normally have me glued to my seat, but I was antsy and instead got up and went out onto the balcony with a glass of cognac to take in the sights.

Neon filled the horizon for as far as I could see. Down below, car horns tooted at each other as The Strip filled with visitors driving in for the weekend from California, Arizona, and faraway places.

I reflected on my three years out in the desert and wondered how things were back in Boston. I supposed the Beantown police force was getting along fine without me. I had left a lot of good friends, lost loves, and too many tragic memories behind, but I wasn't interested in going back any time soon.

I didn't like the direction my reflections were headed, so I gulped back the rest of the drink, left the glass on a patio table, and went back inside.

Just as I returned to the sofa, the bedroom doors parted and out she stepped, wrapped comfortably in one of the Oasis Hotel's white terrycloth bathrobes. Her hair was up and the floral perfume hit my olfactory senses and tripped my heart rate to about 140 bpm.

"Excuse my appearance, Jake," she apologized. "But I thought we'd order up some food and then I'd get changed into something more comfortable."

"You look fine. Besides, what could be more comfortable than a thick, warm robe?"

She picked up the room service menu, smiled, and said, "A thick, warm man."

The old bpm shifted higher again, and all kinds of dormant things started to stir inside me. I fell back into my old reliable remedy and started naming off the starting quarterbacks for each NFL team. Kyoko picked up the telephone and spoke for a few minutes. I didn't hear a word she had said. Who cared?

"They said they'd be a half-hour, 40 minutes," she said.

"Sounds good," I told her in a calm voice. "What do you want to do until then?"

She walked back to the bedroom doors, turned to face me, and let the robe slip off her shoulders and drop to the floor.

"We're down to 39 minutes," she smiled in all her naked splendor. "Do you think that gives you enough time?"

I was almost speechless. "You are the most exquisite thing I've seen in all my life," I told her, meaning every word. "Thirty-nine minutes? I'm hoping I can make it out of the single digits."

"Oh, is that so? Follow me," she said, entering the bedroom. "I know some geisha tricks that should take care of that problem."

I was glad she didn't see my one-footed drunken stumble as I tried to remove my sock chasing her disappearing nakedness.

A little while later, I lay panting as if I'd just run laps.

"Well," Kyoko giggled. "You *almost* made it out of single digits."

The room looked like a cyclone had gone through. The bed was huge and sturdy, probably a double king, and clothes, pillows, sheets, and blankets lay everywhere. There had been no time, nor desire from either one of us, for foreplay. It had been a wild, passionate, down and dirty, no holds barred affair. No sweet talk, no coos, no soft whispered words of love. Not that it had been quiet. *Au contraire.* I was surprised that the yelling and shouting and cries of "Oh, my God!" hadn't alerted Security. And while I couldn't be certain, I was sure my Tarzan call at the end could have been heard by the animals in the circus part of the show downstairs.

"Holy smoke," I exclaimed. "I think it was the geisha move that did it. I thought you were going to use a preventive action?"

"I know," she said, still giggling behind her hand. "I feel terrible. It's been so long since I've used any of the ancient techniques. I was supposed to apply the *Sleepy Sailor*, but I think I got mixed up in the height of passion and used the *Rocket Launcher* by mistake. Sorry. . . ."

"Well, don't be. The pleasure was all mine."

"Yes," she said, rolling off the bed. She picked up our scattered clothes from the floor and went to the dresser. She rearranged things and draped the clothes over a chair near the window. "I'm going to go clean up. Then it's my turn."

"I've got a few tricks of my own, you know," I called out as she entered the bathroom.

"You better," she answered, and clicked the door shut.

Twenty minutes later, the bathroom door opened, and she re-entered the bed freshly showered and fragrant. The room was totally dark except for the sliver of moonlight coming in through the floor-to-ceiling windows.

"You still awake, Jake-*san*?"

"Are you kidding?" I rolled over and bit lightly on her neck and worked my way to her lobes.

"Mmm. That's nice. But I want you to start down at my toes and work your way up. And don't you dare miss an inch."

"I hadn't planned on missing anything," I told her.

"Good," she said, and sighed. "But give me some blankets. The air conditioning is a little cold after the shower."

There was enough linen to cover a football field. I tossed all the blankets and sheets on top of the bed and tucked her in; then I crawled underneath and worked my way down to her feet.

"I'll have you warm in no time," I boasted.

"Shut up and deal. . . ."

That's what the lady wanted, that's what the lady got. I worked on her pretty little toes and gave each one equal time. The same for both feet and calves. Her skin was satin smooth and tasted delicious. Things must have been going okay because she was constantly moaning and groaning and calling my name. She was in for a real treat now because I was just starting in on the back of her knee and this move never failed to please.

From somewhere outside of the room came the sound of a knock.

Kyoko let out a deep sigh. "Room service. I'll let them in."

She must have pressed a button on the night table, because a few seconds later I heard the rattle of a cart as it entered the suite.

"Just leave it there, thank you," Kyoko called out. "There's a twenty-dollar bill on the foyer table for you."

I couldn't hear the response under the covers, but I clearly heard Kyoko say, "The food can wait. Now, where were we. . . ?"

"Right around here," I answered, running my tongue in tiny circles in the fleshy part behind her left knee.

"Ooh," she squeaked. "Yes."

A moment later, I felt Kyoko's body stiffen and gasp. I was about to ask her if she wanted more, when I heard her shout, "What are you doing here?"

I froze. Oh, Christ, I thought to myself. If that was Mr. K., even I couldn't bullshit my way out of this one. All my senses became acutely attuned.

"I told you to leave —"

Someone answered softly from the bedroom doorway, what sounded like "tissue *sayonara*," and Kyoko spat something back vehemently in Japanese. An awkward moment of silence followed, and then a high-pitched thud and whoosh sounded from behind me, and I felt Kyoko go slack.

What the hell was that? My body began to tense and the hairs down the nape of my neck bristled. *That sounded like a goddamn —* Two more thuds resonated, these coming from up in front and to my right, close to the top of the bed. I suddenly realized I'd been holding my breath and let out a quiet stream of air and then took a few short breaths back in. My forehead and back broke out in sweat.

Drawers and cabinets were flung open and I heard things being thrown around from all areas of the bedroom. At one point, a light flashed and I could have sworn it sounded like a picture being taken. I didn't dare make a move. Apparently whoever was tossing the place hadn't noticed me under the blankets and I meant to keep it that way. I felt a cool breeze on my right foot and brought it slowly under the cover. Fortunately, the room was still in virtual darkness.

After what seemed like hours but was probably only a minute or two, the banging and breaking of things ceased. I held my breath. A moment later I heard the clicking of the front door, and then just me gasping for air.

I crept down from under the covers until all of me ended up on the floor. I got up off my knees and scurried around to the top of the bed and toward Kyoko.

"Please say something," I whispered.

Nothing.

The last thing I wanted to do was switch the bed lamp on, but that's what I did. Kyoko stared wide-eyed at the ceiling, mouth agape in alarm. A single black hole just off-center of her forehead told me all I needed to know. I looked for the other two and found them spread an inch apart on her left temple. Dark red blood was oozing onto the bright white pillowcases.

"Ah, shit," I said, and reached for the phone.

Chapter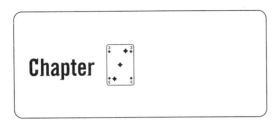

The first call I made was to Security. I explained that there had been a shooting and to monitor all the exits for anyone suspicious; the suspect very likely an Asian male.

The next call was to my old acquaintance, Lieutenant Oakley, Homicide Division. He wasn't at the office, but after explaining the dire circumstances, I persuaded the desk sergeant to call Oakley at home and give him my name and my number here in the suite.

I found my clothes and got dressed, then I went to open the suite to let the soon-to-be procession of people in. When I rounded the doorway of the bedroom and was able to see around the room service cart, my heart took another leap. A young waiter lay face down in the foyer, deep in a pool of his own blood from a deep cut to the throat. A six-inch hunting knife lay next to the body. The killer had to have been quick and strong to take down such a formidable target; the unlucky kid was at least six-two and weighed in about 220.

The phone rang. I didn't want to take the call where I had to look at Kyoko, so I went to the living room to answer.

It was Lieutenant Oakley. "Hey, Morgan, thanks for returning my call so quick."

"What are you talking about?" I asked. "I was calling you."

"You were calling me? I just left a message on your cell phone a half-hour ago."

"Well, then you must have ESP."

"No, I need a favor."

"Well, I got a bigger problem. I need a homicide detective." I gave him a brief explanation of what had happened.

"I don't friggin' believe it," bellowed Oakley's voice from the other end. "What the hell is it with you and people dying? You're like some damned plague."

I let him rant for a minute; then I told him, "Yeah, but don't forget, I almost got whacked, too, a couple of times."

"Un-frickin'-believable," said Oakley, and then after a moment added, "Okay, you know the drill."

"Yeah. Don't touch anything, don't go anywhere. Don't let anyone at the scene except for the ME."

"I'll be there in 20 minutes."

♠

He made it in 18.

The medical examiner, a big man with a Hungarian accent and disheveled gray hair, came in about two minutes later. A couple of serious young assistants, who could have been students, trailed in his wake. They squatted by the waiter and discussed his demise until their knees got sore. Then Oakley and the three of them went into the bedroom, while I mingled with a couple of uniform cops in the living room. I tried to make small talk and they did their best to ignore me. In about five minutes, the doc and the lieutenant came out. The room had filled with more uniforms, suits, and hotel security staff.

"A slit jugular and three to the head," said the examiner to Oakley.

"Boy, this guy's good," I feigned.

"Wait for me out in the hall," snapped Oakley. He went off to talk to some hotel people and I did as I was told.

A few minutes later, the big cop came barreling out the door and walked to the next suite down the hall. He inserted a pass card and held the door open.

"Inside, Shamus," he instructed.

I entered the suite. It, too, was palatial, but this one was designed in a Polynesian motif. Oakley pointed to the group of bamboo chairs. "Sit down."

He took a chair across from me, pulled out his notepad, and picked up the receiver of a nearby telephone. He punched some numbers and a moment later said, "It's me, Oakley. I'm across the hall in 2222. When O'Connor arrives, send him over here." He hung up the phone.

"Okay, Morgan," he sighed, looking at his watch, noting the time, and writing it in his notepad. "Let's begin at the beginning."

And so I did, starting with McClusky coming up to me while I was dealing and telling me to rack up Mrs. K.'s chips. Oakley looked up at me a couple of times while I recited, and once he even stopped writing and raised an eyebrow.

"Had you been hitting on her?" Oakley asked.

"Christ, no. It wasn't anything like that. She's married to some gazil-lionaire back in Japan. She was just here blowing off some steam and having some fun. She'd been kidding around at the poker table, you know, innuendos and such. I made nothing of it until McClusky asked me to spend some time with her."

"But that didn't mean banging her?"

"Of course not. It was like I said; she's here in Vegas, all alone, and just wanted some company, I guess. Dinner, a couple of drinks, share some conversation."

"Yeah, I've always thought of you as the last of the great raconteurs."

We stared at each other for a second and then Oakley said, "Okay, so you took her chips up to her?"

"Chip. I cashed her rack in for a $5,000 single orange chip. From McClusky."

"And where is this chip?"

"I gave it to Kyoko, uh, Mrs. K. The deceased."

Oakley scribbled something in his notepad.

"Right. So introductions are made, you have a couple drinks, she orders some grub, and while you're waiting for it to arrive, the two of you play mommy/daddy. So far, so good?"

"Yeah, but she had a bath in between the ordering and the, uh. . . ."

Oakley checked his book. "Right. Then she goes back to the bathroom to tidy herself up before dinner. The two of you start fooling around again, and that's when she lets room service in?"

"Uh-huh."

"And at this point, you are preoccupied?"

"Yeah. . . ."

"Under the blankets?"

I nodded my head and then Oakley shook his.

"Okay, I get the picture. Then she called out, the guy said something in what sounded like Japanese, and three suppressed shots followed."

"Yup."

"Could you understand any of what the shooter said?"

"Not really. Something about a tissue, then the only word I knew: *sayonara*."

"And that's all you could decipher?"

"It was all Greek to me."

"I thought you said it was Japanese, bright bulb."

"It was. That was just an express — shit! You just reminded me. There was some kind of bright light after the shots were fired. Like maybe a photo flash, or something."

That definitely got Oakley's attention. "You mean the shooter might have taken a picture?"

"Yeah, might have."

The lieutenant was deep in thought.

"What are you thinking?" I asked. "That the guy takes a photo for a trophy?"

"He might . . . or he needs it for proof. Part of the invoice."

Now he had my attention. "Are you saying it might have been a hit?"

Oakley jotted some notes in his book.

"All right, so the room gets tossed, the place is ransacked, and all the while you're still playing hide 'n' seek under the sheets?"

"What can I say? It's a big bed. There was enough linen in there to hide a small army."

"Hmm. . . ." Oakley pondered his notes. "There's a couple of jewelry boxes left empty in the suite. This is going to be quite the haul, I think."

"She was known to be seen wearing a couple hundred thousand in baubles most of the time. Minus her wedding rings, these days."

While he was contemplating, and to change the subject for just a minute, I asked him, "So what were you calling me about?"

"Huh?"

"You said you left me a message."

"Oh, that. Right." He wiped one of his big paws across his face and rubbed at the back of his head. "Yeah, I needed a favor for this Saturday. You were the first one I thought of."

"What kind of favor?"

"I need a dealer."

I gave him a surprised look. "You need a poker dealer?"

"Yeah. We're having this get-together for one of the guys. He's retiring and we were going to have some casino games as part of the festivities."

"And you called me this late? It's Thursday and you want me for the long weekend? Why now?"

"Well, we had a guy, but he was . . . uh, well, he was busted the other day. Got caught selling coke at the casino where he works."

"The dealer was dealin'? So now you need me at the last minute?"

"I checked with the Oasis. You're off this weekend."

"It's a Saturday for God's sake!"

"And I know you have no social life. . . ."

He had a point there. "Look, I just want to play cards this weekend, not deal."

"Ah, come on, Morgan. It's gonna be at headquarters. There's going to be lots of nice police-lady types there, from the field and the offices."

I was shocked. "I'm not looking for love, Oakley. The last one I got involved with just got shot."

"Get real, Morgan. That wasn't love. There was no involvement. She was pissed off at her old man and she was using you to get back at him. Happens thousands of times a day in this city. You were just a tool. A one-night stand."

The seductive effects of the Scotch had long worn off and it was hard to argue.

"You know, Morgan, it wouldn't hurt for you to meet somebody in this town who isn't out to use you, abuse you, or hustle you out of everything you own. Not that you actually own anything, mind you, but you know what I mean."

"I've got the Bugatti," I argued.

"True. That's a beautiful automobile. Why not come out, deal a bit, meet some of our single sisters on the LVMPD, and maybe have someone to share that vehicle with on a leisurely drive down The Strip?"

Police, police women, and police stations all had unpleasant memories for me. I'd worked hard the past three years to brick them in at the back of my brain and I wasn't about to allow a crack in my defenses anytime soon.

"Lieutenant, I'd love to help you out, but the answer is no. Thanks for thinking of me, though."

There was a sharp knock on the door, and the lieutenant worked his way out of the confines of the chair. He turned the handle and another suit walked in, this one in his mid-50s, and Oakley pointed him in my direction.

"Morgan, this is Detective Paul O'Connor. He's going to —"

"I know, I know. He's going to go over the whole thing again with me."

"Just to be sure. I know you understand."

I did. But it didn't mean I had to like it. I fell back into my uncomfortable chair, brought my hands to my face, and made a steeple with my fingers.

Oakley said something to the other cop and left the room.

"Okay," said O'Connor, looking around at the rattan furniture and settling on a bar stool instead. "Why don't we take it from the top?"

And I did.

Lieutenant Oakley re-entered the suite just as I was telling O'Connor how I found the waiter's body in the foyer.

"How's it going, Paul?" asked Oakley.

O'Connor flipped back a few pages in his notebook. "I think I got it all," he said. "And except for a couple of things, I guess most of it makes sense." He glanced at me and then up at Oakley. "Unless you wanna make this guy guilty. . . ."

The lieutenant shook his head. "Sometimes, I wonder if I should. He keeps coming back like a bad penny."

"Ha, ha, ha," I said. "You two guys are as funny as a train wreck."

O'Connor was new to my candor. "Watch it, punk," he warned.

"Oh, gee," I feigned. "Now I'm all confused. Which one of you is supposed to be the good cop?"

"Tell you what, dickhead," O'Connor said, sliding off the stool. "I'll be the *real* bad cop."

Oakley let out a laugh to break the tension. "Paul, I was just kidding around. This guy, you're right, he can be a bit of a dickhead, but he did play cop back on *Boston Vice* until a few years ago."

O'Connor stood there studying me. "What'd you do? Lose your shield in a card game?"

I was shocked at how close to the truth he was, but didn't show it. "Something like that. . . ."

"Figures," he said.

Lieutenant Oakley spent the next few minutes telling O'Connor about the Valentine case and the recent Bonello crime family discovery I'd been involved in. If he was impressed, he didn't express it.

"Look, ladies," I told them. "If you got what you need, I think I'll be going now."

Oakley glanced at O'Connor. "Paul?"

The older cop gave me a look that told me he'd like to cut me down to size. "Well, now that you mention it, Lieutenant. There were a couple of questions I had about the timing of everything, and all."

"Like what?" asked Oakley.

O'Connor stepped up beside him and held out his black notebook.

They conferred in quiet tones, O'Connor pointed with his pen at the page, and Oakley nodded. "Huh, I see what you mean, Paul. It does look a little strange. . . ."

"What are you guys talking about?" I asked. "What looks strange?"

The two of them ignored me. They looked from the lieutenant's big wristwatch and back to the notebook a few times; then they looked at each other and smiled.

"Well, goddamn . . ." snickered O'Connor.

I knew I hadn't killed Mrs. K., so I couldn't figure out what the big deal was.

"What?"

The older cop held up a hand. "Allow me, Lieutenant."

Oakley just shook his head.

"It's the timing," O'Connor explained. "Look at this page. You say she came out of her bath, made a call to room service, and invited you into her bedroom."

"That's how it happened."

"Then the two of you were, uh, intimate?"

"Yes."

"And when it was all over, she went into the bathroom and came out about 20 minutes later."

"You take real good notes," I told him.

"Well, that's just it," said O'Connor, with a smirk on his face. "If room service said 40 minutes, she took 20 minutes in freshening up, and you had been fooling around under the blanket for 10 or 12 minutes when the shooter came in. . . ."

I didn't like where this was leading to.

O'Connor looked over at Oakley, who said, "That only leaves about eight minutes or so for you to have been intimate with the victim, maybe less if you take into account getting undressed and all. Gee, throw in even a little bit of foreplay . . . it doesn't sound like much of a lovemaking session."

I crossed my arms and my ankles, and tried desperately not to defend myself.

O'Connor took over. "You must be real quick on the trigger, pardner," he quipped.

I fixed my eyes on a spot on the wall.

"A regular Don Juan," the older cop added.

Even though this was a murder investigation, Oakley seemed to be enjoying my discomfort. I knew what it was like. I'd been guilty of it myself. Gallows humor was very common in police work, and especially so in the forensics end.

"Christ, Morgan," the lieutenant said. "Don't you know any sports statistics or anything to take your mind off things?"

Of course I did. While my little encounter with Mrs. K. was getting started, I had already gone through the entire list of starting NFL quarterbacks.

"Have you guys ever heard about the *Rocket Launcher*?" I blurted out.

They looked at me like I was some kind of madman, then the two of them burst out laughing.

"It's a geisha technique," I tried to explain.

"Six minutes?" asked O'Connor. "Some technique."

I wasn't about to go through the whole scenario for these two.

"All right," I said. "Enough is enough. Unless you're going to cite me for speeding in a bedroom zone, I think I'm going to go get some fresh air."

Oakley and O'Connor laughed together.

"Well, at least I can tell you were a cop," said the older detective.

That sort of surprised me, but shouldn't have. In the brotherhood of police enforcement, you were expected to take smack as well as you gave it.

"By the way, Morgan," the lieutenant said casually, almost friendly-like. "What did you do with the lady's chip? The $5,000 orange one."

"What are you talking about? I told you, I gave it to her as soon as I got there."

"Hmm."

"What do you mean, 'hmm'?"

"I just went back there and searched the whole suite. There's no orange chip."

I thought about that for a moment. "There has to be. Unless. . . ."

"Unless the perp took it," said Oakley.

"Or our little *ear*-witness here did," offered O'Connor.

"Ah, Christ. . . ."

O'Connor bristled. "Empty your pockets."

"What the hell?" I countered. "Are you saying — ?"

Oakley stepped in again. "Just do it, Jake. At least this way there's no question."

It was only the second time since I'd known Oakley that he called me by my first name, so I reluctantly complied. I dug into my pants pockets and placed keys, coins, and other guy stuff on the coffee table.

"There," I said when I'd finished.

O'Connor went through my things and Oakley went to a telephone and made a call.

"Okay, arms out," said the detective.

"What?" I asked incredulously. "You're going to frisk me?"

"You know the drill, Morgan. Just do as you're told."

"Un-friggin'-believable . . ." I said, holding my arms out from my sides.

O'Connor patted me down from my shirt collar to my socks.

"Take off the shoes," he instructed.

I pursed my lips and kicked off my loafers.

"Let me see your feet."

I dropped back in my chair and put my legs up. "Don't you dare tickle."

O'Connor felt around and finally gave up. He walked over to the bar sink and washed his hands. "Nothing," he told the lieutenant.

"So, if O'Connor here is finished with his fetishes, can I go?" I asked.

There was a knock at the door.

"Soon," said Oakley. He walked over and let the visitor in.

"You called, Lieutenant?" It was the medical examiner and his two wannabes.

"Yeah, thanks for coming by, Boris."

"Is that him?"

"Yup."

"I see," said the doctor. "And we are looking for?"

"A casino chip," chirped in O'Connor.

"Ah," the medical examiner said, and his minions nodded their heads in unison.

I raised a bushy eyebrow. "Uh, guys . . . what the hell is going down here exactly?"

"I'm sorry." Oakley was all business. "But we've gotta be sure."

"Yeah," agreed O'Connor, leaning against the bar and crossing his arms with a stupid smirk on his face.

A sudden realization smacked me across the forehead. "Hold on a minute!" I exclaimed. "You don't mean what I think you mean, do you?"

"Lieutenant?" asked the doctor, in his heavy accent. "You ask me for favor. But I must get this done as soon as possible. I have busy night. There's drowning at spa across street and drive-by up north with three people shot."

"Sure thing. And I appreciate it." Oakley looked over at me. "It'll just take a minute, Morgan. Get in the washroom, drop your pants, bend over, and hang onto the sides of the sink."

"But Lieutenant . . ." I pleaded.

The medical examiner reached into his jacket pocket, pulled out a latex glove, and as he placed it on his right hand with a snap, I couldn't help but notice how long and thick his fingers were.

Chapter

"But you know, Morgan," reflected Oakley, with a strange smirk on his face. "If a friend did a special favor for another friend, the one getting the favor should really trust the other one if he says he has nothing hidden on his person. . . ."

I stared down Oakley for about 20 seconds and gave him my best *You-son-of-a-bitch!* look. "What time Saturday do you need me?"

"Eight o'clock will be fine," smiled the lieutenant. "It'll give you time to mingle."

"Yeah," I said, still smarting from his persuasive powers. "I really want to mingle with your kind."

"So," barked the medical examiner, snapping off his rubber glove. "I take it you won't be needing my services after all?"

Oakley put an arm around the big doctor and walked him and his cronies to the door. When he came back, he slapped his hands together and said, "Okay, where were we?"

"The chip," O'Connor reminded him.

"Oh, yeah. How could I forget?"

"Very funny," I told him.

"We do what we have to do," said Oakley. "But you know as well as I do that a $5,000 chip is not that easy to pass these days. Pardon the pun. With all the worry about homeland security and being careful with foreign money being laundered through Vegas via the Mid East, everybody is on the lookout."

"And not just anybody can cash it, either," I added. "Which is why I wouldn't have taken it even if I could have. Every token $5,000 and bigger has been numbered and microchipped. You can't have somebody else cash it in for you either. Even if they buy it off you at 10 cents to the dollar, they're going to get scrutinized by the gaming commission, IRS, DEA, and a whole bunch of other acronyms."

"So that chip would have been documented when it was taken out," stated O'Connor.

"Yeah," I agreed. "It would have. I recorded it under McClusky's name. Find the chip, and you probably have your killer."

"Pretty much," concurred Oakley, but I could tell he had something else on his mind.

O'Connor shook his head. "Morgan, when this hits the papers, you'll probably be some kind of hero for surviving this whole thing. Even though you were hiding the whole time."

"Hiding? Yeah, right. I was surviving for Christ's sake. What'd you expect me do? Get him in a pillow fight? And by the way, I'm not looking for any press. I've had enough attention in this town over the past year to last me a lifetime, thank you very much."

We could both see the lieutenant was deep in thought. "You know," he finally said. "I'm thinking maybe we should keep Morgan out of this, for now."

"Why's that?" asked the other cop.

"Well, whoever the shooter was, once they find out there was somebody else there. . . ."

Now he had me wondering.

"You think they might come back for Speedy Gonzalez here?"

Oakley was still pondering. "They might. They can't be sure what Morgan heard or saw. If it was just a robbery, big deal, who'd care? But we've got two dead bodies and one more won't make much difference."

It would to me! I thought but didn't say.

"There's another way to look at it," offered O'Connor. "We could promote it in all the media that there was a witness, that maybe he even has some information. That way, we might flush the killer out into the open when he comes after Morgan."

"Uh, excuse me, boys?" I interrupted. "But do I get a say in any of this?"

Oakley thought about it for a moment; then he said, "That's got merit, but for now, let's go with the hushed-up version. See how it plays."

"Yeah," said O'Connor. "I guess so. At least until after Saturday's party."

Chapter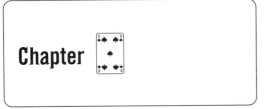

It was just after 7:30 on Saturday night, and I was driving north on I-15 on my way to the Downtown Area Police Command facility on 9th Street. I'd spent a good portion of the past two days watching the news and reading newspaper articles on the murder of Mrs. K. All of the reports cited robbery as the apparent motive. A distraught Mr. Kobayashi had arrived that morning and confirmed what many had suspected — that his wife's traveling jewelry collection would probably have exceeded half a million dollars.

A tough way to make a living: taking two lives and getting five to seven percent by trading the goods to a fence. But then again, I hate to think of how many people have been knocked off in the past for a lot less than $25,000.

The news said police were going over videotapes from the Oasis' security team, but because of the extensive number of cameras located throughout the casino, elevators, hotel floors, and exterior, the task would take days, if not weeks.

And it wasn't the only high-profile case the Vegas cops had to work on that day; over the past year and a half, there had been a rash of large-item robberies — from wealthy visitors and even a number of local celebrities — yet to be solved. Making matters even worse, there had been at least a dozen cases where someone had been killed for what was stolen.

I pulled into the busy lot of the command facility and took pleasure in taking up two spaces parking my pride and joy. It was the big, black, pristine 1939 Bugatti Type 57 I was given by the family of ex-Vegas crime boss Carmine Bonello last fall for my part in unraveling his 50-year-old murder — complete with bullet holes.

Inside, a gruff desk sergeant directed me to the east wing, which he described as the recreation area. He told me it housed an extensive athletic department and I was to follow the directions to the gymnasium. I thanked him with a shot from my finger gun and he looked like he wanted to pull out his Glock and return fire. Perhaps he hadn't been invited to the party.

I walked the long gray corridor, skirting busy office staff members and uniformed cops, and glancing at pictures and portraits of officers honored for their outstanding achievements, and those who had been tragically taken in the line of duty.

I followed the signs and eventually came to a set of double doors from which lots of noise was coming. Behind a little wooden table a young female uniform was sitting, talking to a woman standing nearby in a pinstriped pantsuit. The uniform was checking off names on a sheet of paper while the suit stood there giving me the once-over. She was somewhere in her mid-30s, an inch or two shy of my six feet, with an athletic build, and dark brown hair pulled back into a business-like do. She had dramatic green eyes and was wearing the minimum in makeup. An understated woman who knew what she wanted and how to go about getting it. The kind of gal I'd normally try to take a shot at if I wasn't still a little shook up over Mrs. K.

"Ticket?" she asked, looking me right in my baby blues.

"Sorry," I told her, glancing down at the red tag on her jacket that said: *Hello, my name is Laura.* "I don't have one."

"That'll be $25, then."

"Actually, I'm part of the hired help."

She studied me again and her cute little brows went up. "Really?" she asked. "You sure look like a cop."

I smiled and nodded. "I get that a lot," I explained. "I'm ex. From back East."

"Well, good," she said. "If it's one thing I know, it's cops. For a second there, I thought I was losing my touch."

"No, you've still got it," I said. "Are you one of the office staff?"

The uniform looked up at the suit and suppressed a laugh.

"Not exactly," she said, and extended a hand. "I'm a detective. Metro Vice."

I took her hand, surprised at the power of her grip.

"My name's Laura," she announced politely.

"Already figured that out," I told her. "I was a detective, too, you know."

She let go of my hand, and gave me a friendly slap on the shoulder. I must have been slightly off balance, because she rocked me pretty good.

"Don't give me that crap," she said and laughed out loud. "You read the name tag. Wow, some detective."

"Well. . . ."

"So what's your name?"

"Jake," I told her. "Jake Morgan."

Laura and the uniform read down the list. "There's no Morgan here," she said.

"I was sort of a last-minute replacement. I'm supposed to deal cards for a poker game. Lieutenant Oakley arranged it all."

A few other people had arrived in the line and were patiently waiting to hand in their tickets.

"Wait out here, will you?" Laura asked. "I'll just be a minute."

I stepped aside. "You can never be too careful," I told her.

She patted me on the back as she walked around me, but this time I was ready for her and stood my ground. "You got that right, Jake. And I'm a very, very careful gal."

I walked around and read a bunch of framed citations on the walls and looked at some photos of various Vegas police teams competing in tug-of-war and feats of strength. One of the guys pulling a police car and a paddy wagon across a finish line looked a lot like Lieutenant Oakley.

"Yeah, that's him."

I turned, and there was Oakley with Laura.

"So, he's okay?" she asked.

The lieutenant wiggled a finger at me to come over. "That's debatable in some circles. But, yeah, he's here to deal tonight."

"Good," said Laura. "He looks like an interesting guy."

"Oh, Jake's an interesting guy, all right," Oakley said, slapping me on the back, but with less force than Laura. "Whatever he touches ends up in bad luck or murder."

"Come on, that's not entirely —"

"Well, I may have to find out for myself," replied Laura with a seductive smile.

Oakley shook his head and laughed. "Laura, you're as tough as they come, but you're asking for trouble with this one. He's high maintenance and low bank account."

Laura stood there judging me with interest.

"I hate to break up this little party," said the lieutenant, "but I have to get Jake over to the poker table to deal."

"Nice to meet you," I told the girls.

"Likewise," said Laura. "Maybe we'll meet up again later."

Lieutenant Oakley and I entered the cavernous gymnasium area. There were two basketball courts separated by a retractable vinyl wall and wooden bleachers around the entire court area. About 100 people mingled in animated conversation, nibbling finger food from Styrofoam plates and drinking punch from clear plastic cups. A train of six uniformed officers came by carrying three big basins of beer in ice on their way to the bar. Oakley reached into one of the tubs, grabbed two wet Coors, and handed me one. He cracked the cap open and pointed the business end of the bottle over to the far corner.

"The poker table is over there," he said. "And don't forget, you're working on tips. You can sip a few free brewskies while you're on the job tonight, but don't get shit-faced. You don't want to be pulled over for DUI in the police parking lot."

"I'll be good," I told him, and then took a healthy slug of beer.

"You better," Oakley warned. "You're here on my recommendation."

"Don't worry, I won't embarrass you," I said, followed by a belch that rang out like a gunshot and could be heard halfway across the room. When people turned to look at the culprit, I pointed to the lieutenant.

"You see what I mean?" said Oakley.

"Oh, come on. I'm just kidding around." I pointed at a huge red and white banner strung against the far wall. "So who's Bull?" I asked.

Oakley took a swig from his bottle. "That's who we're here honoring tonight. Captain Alexander Bulloch. Better known as The Bull. He's retiring."

The moniker struck a chord in the back of my brain. "Name sounds familiar."

"Yeah, that's right. You're a detective," Oakley said with a smile. "You just met his niece, Laura."

She hadn't given me a last name when we met. "No, I remember reading about him in the paper a while ago. Some kind of big narco bust or something involving one of the casinos."

"That would be The Bull," Oakley said proudly. "Twenty-five years of battling the streets of Vegas gets you a lot of press. Good and bad. In another four to six weeks, he'll just be another citizen of our fine city."

The room was filling up quickly and the noise level was rising with it. "Nice turnout."

Oakley looked around. "Yup. There's the mayor chatting to the governor. The chief speaking to a couple of judges. Oh, and there's The Bull being interviewed by Channel 8."

I glanced over to where he was pointing and there he was talking to a reporter and cameraman. He appeared to be in his late 50s, perhaps early 60s, average height and weight, yet distinguished looking. He wore a dark blue suit as if he was born to, and his dark, wavy hair was just turning to silver at the temples. Women would say he was aging well.

Up on a small stage some technician was playing around with a microphone at a dais. He kept tapping the mic and telling someone else to turn up the volume until a screech of feedback shot across the room. "Testing, testing, one, two —"

On the count of three, a phalanx of officers in uniforms and suits pelted the techie with buns from the banquet table.

A moment later, Lieutenant Oakley said, "Okay, that's my cue. I'm doing a little emceeing tonight. I'll catch up with you later."

Oakley walked up to the stage, adjusted the microphone stand for his height, and began to speak. He started off by reminding everyone why they were here and led into Bulloch's early years on the force. Somewhere around his move from Traffic into Vice as an eight-year vet, I zoned out and looked around for Laura, but she was nowhere to be found. I even popped my head through the doors to see if she was still taking tickets. No luck.

I wasn't even sure why I was looking for her. This woman looked to have her shit together and carried herself as if she flicked guys off just for the hell of it. She had a great job, a promising career, and an inner poise that just oozed with confidence. But I had always been a sucker for a female in a uniform, even if it was a pantsuit. And unless the old Jakester's gal radar was malfunctioning, he had been a blip on her screen, too.

Oakley mentioned that he was going to be followed by a couple of other dignitaries who were present but had to leave soon. Following their words, the crowd was to enjoy the sumptuous spread of cold cuts and potato salad and sit back and enjoy one of the games of chance. All profits, he explained, would be going to a good cause, which I assumed was probably the police fund.

The beer had gone down rather quickly and, since I knew I'd be sitting for the next few hours, I decided to find a washroom. At this point I was standing near one of the corners and the door to my left said LOCKERS. Why bother going down the hall to look for a washroom? A locker room should have a place for a guy to go, so I slipped inside the doorway and into semi-darkness.

Not so bad. By the light of the occasional emergency bulb, I made my way down the short hallway until I came to a door marked MEN'S LOCKER 2. I tried the handle and the door opened without a sound. I stepped into the darkened room and could make out the rows of metal lockers, slatted wooden benches, and the unmistakable scent of disinfectant, sweat, and the combination of a hundred different colognes and roll-ons. Here too, the occasional emergency light made it just possible to see.

I walked past a large shower room and came to a wooden door with an opaque window. I pushed the door and could just make out a counter of sinks, a long row of urinals, and across from them, metal bathroom stalls. The room was almost pitch-black and I held the door open as I searched for a light switch. No luck. I didn't want to end up working the next few hours with pee spray on my pants, so I grabbed a wooden chair from the locker room and propped it between the door and frame so I could see outlines.

As I was doing what I came to do, I heard voices as somebody entered the far end of the locker room. Two, maybe three, male voices. One, very bass and assertive, was far more dominant and agitated than the others.

"I don't give a fuck! I've had it up to here."

"We all have."

"Yeah? Well, it's time we did something about it."

"So how do you want to handle it?"

Damn. Now I'd gone and got myself in the middle of a police pissing contest, pardon the pun. I quietly finished and did up my zipper, knowing I'd have to lie low. I didn't want any part of their problem and they sure as hell didn't want to involve me.

"How do we handle it? The same way Spooky was handled. With a bullet. How else?"

A bullet? This was more information than I wanted to know. I had just come in for a leak, not to get caught up in some dirty-cop campaign. I thought about sticking a finger in each of my ears and humming a tune but was sure they'd hear me. Instead I turned to wait it out.

As I stepped away, a green LED button, chest high on the ceramic wall, turned to red and the urinal went to auto flush with a godawful loud noise.

"What the fuck?" came from just the other side of the door.

He'd taken the words right out of my mouth.

I wisely forgot about washing my hands for the moment. My eyes had adjusted to the barely lit room and I made out the handle of a broom leaning against the counter and a large waste receptacle. I dropped to my knees and squeezed in to the wall as tightly as I could. Just then, the chair was kicked out of its place and slid into the washroom. It hit one of the sinks and fell over with a crash about two feet in front of me. The urinal I'd been using stopped circulating water suddenly and all was quiet.

A large silhouette with almost no neck filled the doorway. Even with the door wide open, I knew there wasn't much that my intruder could see. Although he might hear my knees knocking. I could see him searching for a switch.

"Anybody got a lamp?" he asked.

"Yeah, right," somebody said. "I got a Maglite in my pants."

"Oh, my," someone else said. "I thought you were just happy to see me."

I used to love cop banter like this when I was on the force back in Boston, but right now I didn't find it at all funny. I might later if I got out of this without getting shot.

"You guys won't think this is so funny if it gets out of our unit." The silhouette took a step inside, still holding the door. "I don't see nobody."

I took hold of the broom handle and slowly lifted it and brought it by the closest urinal. I held it there for about five seconds and then slowly withdrew it. The water started to surge with a noisy splashing sound.

"Ah, hell," said the voice at the door. "There it goes again. Must be on automatic. I can make out the pissers and there's nobody there." He turned and stepped back into the locker room area. "You guys see how jumpy this thing has got me?"

The washroom fell into total darkness. I wasn't in good enough shape to stay crouched down in this tiny, confining space, so I slowly got to my feet, quietly placing the broom back where I'd found it. I stretched for a moment, still aware of the heated voices just outside the door. I glanced down at my left wrist and the luminous hands of my watch told me I was due to start dealing in a couple of minutes.

As much as I didn't want to, the urgency and intrigue of the situation got the better of me. And why not? I'd been a good cop. I'd done enough time in Vice that I couldn't really not do anything about what I'd just heard. I just didn't want to get caught doing it.

I made my way closer to the door and cracked it an inch. The people who belonged to the voices were out of sight around a corner.

"So we're all in agreement?"

"Yeah."

"Me too. But what about Rat?"

"What about him? He's not here and wouldn't matter anyway. It would still be three to one. Majority rules."

"That's the way it's always been."

"You're right, Teddy Bear."

"Okay, so it's a go. We take out Bulloch. For good."

"When and how?"

"Personally, if anyone gets a clear shot and can get away without being seen, I don't care."

"Okay, I agree; we can't make a mistake. It has to be done with no chance of retribution. If we don't do a clean job, you know we're fucked."

"Bulloch will talk for sure."

"No question. And then it's all over for us."

"Well, I'm not taking that chance. If I get the opportunity, it'll be done right. One hundred percent fatal, no eye-wits."

"I wish we could come up with a good 10–66 and keep the heat away."

"That's a best case scenario, for sure. But either way, we are not to be recognized."

"I've been carrying a fucking ski mask around in my car, in Las Vegas for Christ's sake. I'm not taking any chances."

"I don't blame you. Look at the risk for us all."

The other two grunted their agreement and their words trailed off as they walked to the far end of the locker room. Eventually I heard no voices and an eerie silence fell.

My mind was reeling. I had just walked into a hornet's nest and wasn't sure what exactly I should do. It looked like the honored guest of tonight's affair was in deep shit and I had the inside scoop. I guessed I should tell Oakley about what I had heard, seeing as he seemed to be pretty close to The Bull. And maybe that way I could wash my hands of the whole thing.

That reminded me, and I propped the chair in the doorway once again, went over to the sinks, waited as the faucet came on automatically, and cleaned up. As I wiped up with some paper towels, I noticed how nervous I looked in the dimly lit mirror. I didn't actually feel afraid; it was more concerned.

I kept telling myself that, even as I rushed back to the urinal and relieved myself again for the second time in five minutes.

Chapter

"There you are!"

It was Oakley: just the man I wanted to talk to.

"Hey, Lieu —"

"Where the hell you been? I was looking all over for you."

"I was in the washroom. But look, I've gotta tell —"

"Save it for later. There's already a bunch of guys over at the poker table ready to play, so get your ass over there."

"But. . . ."

"Not now. I've gotta meet up with the mayor and walk him out to his car."

With that, he was gone.

♦

"Okay, ladies and gentlemen," I instructed. "The game is $10–$20 No Limit Hold 'Em poker."

Each of the ten players had bought-in for $100 and received $1,000 in poker chips, which I guess was done to make them feel like high rollers. The red chips were worth an imaginary $25 each and the black worth $100 apiece. Since I was working on tips, this wasn't a bad structure. I could normally get in between 50 and 60 hands per hour, and if I got a chip toked every hand, I would pull in at least $100 bucks an hour, tax-free. Not bad.

Still, the little white Jake-angel on my left shoulder said I should track down Oakley and explain to him what I had overheard. A man's life could be at stake, for God's sake. The little red Jake-devil on my right shoulder said screw it, take the money, you've got plenty of time; nobody was going to whack the guy anywhere close to his farewell party, for Satan's sake.

"And," I announced, with great flair and fanfare as I riffled the cards, "as my two ex-wives, current wife, girlfriend, six kids, and Gamblers Anonymous counselor would like to remind everyone, the dealer *does* accept tips. . . . ."

The players laughed in unison and one of them, a large, black, plain-clothes cop, tossed two red chips at me and said, "Okay, here," in a deep tone. "Now shut up and deal." He showed me a wide mouth of pearly white teeth as his lips parted in a smirk.

As I tried to match his smile, I couldn't help but notice how aptly he would fill a washroom doorway in silhouette.

"Okey-dokey," I said, and cut the cards. "Game on."

I started firing cards clockwise around the table, keeping one eye on the game and one out for Oakley.

Over the next three hours, players went bust and new ones filled their seats. There were no real big winners except for me and the house. I had made about $250 in tokes and the house had close to $900 collected for the evening. Oakley came by and told everyone at the table to take a 10-minute break so I could stretch my legs, and for all of us to grab a plate of food to take back for when the game resumed.

I took the opportunity to get Oakley's attention.

"Lieutenant?"

"How's it going, Morgan?" he said, scanning the room.

"Great. Listen, I've got to tell you about this thing I heard. About Bulloch."

"Yup. He's a good man. I bet you heard a lotta good things about him coming from the players at the table."

"Well, yeah, but that's not what I meant."

Some kind of commotion broke out across the gym where a bunch of people were gambling by throwing half-dollars closest to the wall. One of the female meter maids had gotten into a yelling and shoving match with a male cop from the K-9 unit over whose coin was closer.

Oakley shook his head at the situation. "Save the story on Bulloch for later." He instructed one of the cops in uniform to secure the poker table while he went to clear up the fuss. But the parking officer kicked the canine officer square in the crotch and he went down to his knees. A couple of hoorays came up from the crowd.

"Take your break and I'll see you in a little while, Morgan."

As Oakley stomped off to intercede, a rather large German shepherd sprung from his perch on the bleacher, knocked the parking officer to her ass on the floor, and started to pull ferociously at her boot. Now everyone began to point and laugh.

As I turned away from the spectacle to take advantage of my break, I could hear Oakley yelling, "Here doggie. Here's some bologna. Release. Release. Be a good boy."

I went off in search of the washroom, but this time I avoided the locker room area and went straight out the main doors and down the hallway.

Chapter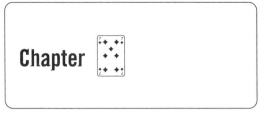

Fifteen minutes later, just after midnight, I was back at the poker table and firing cards around to each of the players. The lieutenant had cooled down the fracas between Parking and K-9 and the sounds of good old-fashioned rock and roll now filled the air. There had only been one player replacement at the table since the break. The pungent odor from the big, sweaty, cigar-smoking guy, who had vacated the seat on my left, had been fortunately replaced with the heavenly scent of lavender and the easy-on-the-eyes Laura the vice cop.

For the next hour, I dealt, she played, and the two of us bantered back and forth while her stack of chips grew. She handled herself well on the poker table for the most part, but the more punch she drank, the more her game and tongue loosened up. Eventually her chips dwindled as the repartee between us increased, but she didn't seem to mind. Her jokes kept the table light and friendly, and her attention to me resulted in my interest in her rising. At one point it struck me that just a few days ago I had left a scenario similar to this with the late Mrs. K. and I marveled at the coincidence. I was certain this development would have a happier ending. As long as Laura didn't pass out.

The music turned softer after 1 a.m., and slowly player after player left the table until we were down to four-handed. The winners had left the losers to chase their losses. Laura had just lost the last of her chips and started to dig around in her purse for more money.

"Ah, Laura," I said. "You really want to re-buy? It's getting kind of late."

"Soooo?" she slowly slurred. "I don't have anywhere to go."

"Hey, dealer," yelled the player wearing an NY-stitched baseball cap. "Mind your own fuckin' business. If the lady wants to play, let her play. It's her money."

Of the four players, Laura was on my immediate left. Player two, the Yankee fan, was two seats to the left of her, around 10 o'clock from my position. Player three was directly across from me, and player four two seats to my right. I looked around for Lieutenant Oakley. I had an uneasy feeling that there might be another ruckus rapidly rising. My pocket was bulging with tokes and I was more than happy to call it a night. And, to be honest, Laura's enticing aroma was still attacking the brain cells responsible for my gallantry.

"Yeah," said the player opposite me, a whiner who blamed everything and everybody for his losing except himself and his own bad play. "Just shut up and deal."

"That's all you're here for," said the first guy. "Deal monkey, deal."

I smiled at all of them the best I could, and I patted Laura's hand to comfort her. As far as I knew, only one of these guys was actually a cop, and he was from Henderson. Of the other two, one was a garage mechanic that helped look after the fleet of vehicles, and the other guy was some kind of loudmouth legal beagle. I took the blue-backed cards we were using, spread them out, and proceeded to rip them in half.

"What the fuck?"

"Whatta you doin'?"

"You asshole!"

"Jake?" That was Laura.

"Don't worry, sweetheart," I reassured her. "I know what I'm doing. I can handle things."

I picked up the extra, red-backed cards from my dealer tray and proceeded to tear up that deck.

"What the hell you doing?"

"Darn," I said, throwing the ripped cards around the table. "It looks like the game is over. We don't have any more cards." I stood and leaned across to the big mouth sitting in front of me. "Too bad."

"Yeah," he replied, getting up from his seat, "too bad for you."

I reached over, grabbed the guy by his shirt, and started to haul him over to my side. Well, that was the plan. Unfortunately, player three cold-cocked me from my blind side, and nailed me with a right cross to the cheek that knocked me over Laura and onto the floor.

"Jake?" screamed Laura.

I sat there for a second until the ceiling lights slowed their spinning and started to converge into each other. "Don't worry, babe," I assured her, wincing as I rubbed my face. "I'll take care of these clowns in a second. As soon as I can focus."

The guy who had hit me came charging. "Yeah? Focus on this."

I saw two images of Laura leap from her seat, use the table for a brace, and jump in the air. Before the guy coming at me knew it, her right foot came flicking out and her instep caught him with a perfect round-house kick. His head snapped back, his eyes rolled up, and there he was on the floor with me. Except he was asleep.

Laura let her momentum carry her up and over my chair and onto the table itself. The guy I had tried to tug over the table stood there with his mouth open. Laura landed in front of my tray with her back to him. In one motion, she bent down, spun around, and drop-kicked him square on the jaw. He joined the rest of us on the hardwood floor.

My head began to clear a bit and I remembered there was a third guy, just as he dove over the table and pulled her legs out from under her. She landed on her back with a thud and let out a rush of air from her lungs.

"Ah, hell," I said, trying to get up to help her. I did get up, but then everything started to spin again and I tipped over. "I'll be right there, Laura."

She had a weird smile on her face as the Yankee fan straddled her hips, pinned her arms, and bent over like he was going to kiss her. He got about four inches from her lips when she drove forward and head-butted him. The guy's hat flew off and he let go of her wrists to check if his skull had split. With no sign of blood, he sneered at her and brought both hands down, aimed directly for her throat.

There was pure evil in his eyes. "You rotten —"

As his fingers spread to choke her, she brought her hands up and slapped his arms away and out to his sides. He reared back and Laura didn't waste a second. She flipped her body up into the air, spread both legs, and scissor-locked the guy's head between her thighs, the left side of his head resting in her crotch. She held him firmly in that position as they both lay on the table. By this time, a crowd had joined us and formed a circle.

His face started to change color as the lack of oxygen to his brain took effect. Laura sat back with her arms behind her and seemed to monitor her prey's breathing and coloration. As his hands fell feebly to the table, and his body began to shake, Laura eased the pressure of her muscular thighs and released her victim. He fell back onto the table but did not move. Laura rolled off the side and walked up to him. She put two fingers to his neck and monitored his pulse, then she lifted his eyelid for a look.

"He'll be okay," Laura announced as she walked over to me and helped me up.

Some of the crowd had revived the first two attackers and they were sitting in chairs at the poker table. One of the onlookers poured a pitcher of water onto the last guy and he sputtered and floundered like a fish on shore.

"Wow," I said, as Laura checked my face. "Cool moves."

"Yeah," she said, and held a finger in front of my face. "Okay, tough guy, follow my finger." She moved it left and right, up and down, and eventually proclaimed me fit.

"That was a helluva leg lock," I told her.

"Four years of Thigh Master," she bragged with a smile. "Suzanne Somers has nothing on me."

"You're a regular hellcat," I said. "Like those guys on *Ultimate Fighter*."

"You about ready?" she asked.

"For what?"

"To get out of this place."

"Hey, you two," came a booming voice. "What's going on?"

It was Lieutenant Oakley. The cavalry had arrived. Late as usual.

"Oh, hi," said Laura.

I just nodded and checked the inside of my mouth for loose teeth.

Oakley looked around at the mess. "What happened?"

"Ah, nothing," I told him. "Just a few sore losers."

"Very sore," Laura said.

"Okay," announced the lieutenant. "Things look as if they're wrapping up around here for the night anyway. I'm going to close down the games."

He went and cleaned out the tray of its raked money from the pots. "Not bad," he said. "There's about $1,300 here. What did you make in tips?"

"I did pretty good," I said, pulling chips from my pockets and placing them on the table.

Oakley stacked my green chips in piles of fours, which in real money was piles of tens. The blacks were stacked in five to a pile, which was 50 bucks to me. "Very good," he said proudly. "You've got $360 here."

"Thank you," I said.

"No, no, thank *you!*" Oakley began splitting the chips in half. When he was finished he slid half the pile my way.

"What's this?" I asked incredulously.

"Your tips."

"What about those?" I said, pointing at the stacks he had taken.

"Those are the donation."

"What donation?"

"You know," explained Oakley. "Where all the profits are going. Believe me Morgan, it's a good cause."

"But I thought you said I was working on tips."

"You were. But come on, with the chip structure the way it was, we knew it would be way out of line." He gave me a fatherly look. "Don't you think close to 400 bucks for a few hours work is a little excessive? Especially for a charity-type event?"

I just shook my head. "You guys are worse than the IRS."

"Ah, come on, Morgan. Admit it. You had a good time." He glanced over at Laura, who was stretching her long legs after her workout. "Met some nice people."

"Okay, okay," I laughed. "Where do I cash in my portion?"

Oakley grinned. "Over there, that little window by the hot dog stand."

I saw where he was pointing and told Laura I'd be right back.

"Wait a sec," said the lieutenant. "What about that thing you wanted to talk to me about?"

"That's right. That thing." I didn't really want to discuss what I had to say in front of her. "Would you mind if I talked to the lieutenant, Laura?"

"No problem," she said, as she turned to leave. "I'm going to go freshen up. Be back in five."

I watched her as she walked away. It was a tremendous walk.

"For Christ's sake, Morgan," extolled Oakley with a big sigh. "Do you have any idea what you're getting yourself into?"

"I hope so. I think so. I'm just not sure why."

"Now don't get me wrong. She's a terrific gal and a fine cop. I knew her parents, too. But she has a rep of going through guys the way you go through a paycheck. And if you screw her over, look out. She'll neuter you mentally and physically."

I had to laugh. "She's still a girl, if you haven't noticed. Okay, she's taken a little bit of martial arts, and can handle herself in a fight, but she still wears heels and carries a purse with tissue inside so she can clear a tear at a tender moment."

"Well, don't say I didn't warn you," sighed Oakley. "Now forget about your hormones for a minute and tell me what was so urgent about Bulloch?"

"Oh, right," I told him. "When I first got here, I was someplace I wasn't supposed to be and overheard some things I wasn't supposed to hear."

"That's my boy, Morgan. Go on."

"Well, there were three of them, I think, one of them a big guy with a deep voice. They were talking about how pissed off they were with Bulloch and how they'd have to take care of him."

"Maybe they were talking about dumping a cooler of Gatorade on him tonight like football players do to their coach."

"No, they said he was interfering with things and they couldn't afford to have him talk. They said they were going to have to make it permanent. With a bullet."

Now I seemed to have Oakley's interest.

"They said that? With a bullet?"

"Yup."

The lieutenant thought about that for a moment, then he shook his head. "It just doesn't make any sense," he said. "The guy is retiring in a month. It's his party. Why the hell would anyone be pissed off at the guy when they weren't going to be seeing him again?"

I shrugged my shoulders. "Beats me. That's just what I heard and I thought you should know."

Oakley nodded. "You did the right thing. I'll have a word with The Bull. See if any of this makes sense to him."

"Good," I said. "Because if the truth be known, I don't want any part of a police pissing contest. I told you what I know, and I wash my hands of the affair. Now, if you don't mind, I'll be cashing in what little you left me."

"Yeah," he said, although his mind seemed elsewhere. "I appreciate the info."

A thought struck me. "Appreciate it enough to give me back the so-called donation money you took from me?"

"No," he said, as he looked around the room for The Bull. "Now get lost."

Chapter

At the window, I slid across my stack of $180 in chips to the two ladies behind the counter. One of them, gray haired, slightly hunched, and with a wide smile, reminded me of my aunt Dorothy back in Boston. The other, in her mid-30s, was far too young to be wearing what looked like a permanent sad frown.

"Very nice, sir," said the elderly one. "A very nice win."

"Why thank you, ladies."

"Would you like to contribute?"

"Contribute?"

"To the charity," the second one said, with the trace of a foreign accent.

"Well, you see, it just so happens that I already donated. I was dealing poker. I gave it to Lieutenant Oakley. Honestly, I did; he's right over there."

The older woman smiled and looked at me. That was when I noticed the little tags and black ribbon they wore on their aprons. They read *My loved one died in the line of duty. Please give to our cause.* The friendly one's tag had *In loving memory of Sgt. Terrence Whittaker* etched beneath, and the forlorn one's read: *In loving memory of Det. Vladimir Kasparitis.*

"That's for the policemen's annual function, I think," said the first woman. "We collect for a benevolent group for families who have lost loved ones while on the job; you know, for special grief counselors, financial assistance, things like that."

I had personal experience with losing a police partner, which is probably what made me swallow so hard.

"We give a receipt for all donations, large or small," said the other. "For tax write-offs. Anything you see fit is acceptable."

"How could I not be swayed by two beautiful salesladies like yourselves?" I said.

They both beamed. "Then you'll donate?"

"Sure."

The older one reached for a pen while the other produced a receipt pad. "How much should we make it out for?"

Laura came up and put her arm through mine. "How's my knight in shining armor?" she asked.

I acknowledged her with a bright smile and told the ladies, "Throw in a couple of coffees and you can make the receipt for the whole $180."

"Oh, that's wonderful," said the one writing. When she finished, she leaned in close to the counter and whispered, "You know, sweetie, the coffee is free anyway."

I looked over at Laura and laughed. "I know."

The two of us got our java and sat down at an empty table, listening to one of the cops tinkling the ivories on a piano that had been rolled in. There were still about 50 people milling about, most of them drinking the same thing we were before driving home.

"I have to say," I remarked, after taking a sip of hot brew, "you are one interesting lady."

She gave me a delightful smile, pulled out a cigarette, and lit it. "You should know I don't treat all my men that rough."

"I hope not."

She gave me a playful look as if she was sizing me up. As attracted as I was to her, I had to admit she scared me a bit at the same time. It was weird. No woman had ever affected me in this manner. The thought that perhaps I wasn't in her league, or capable of even trying out for the team, drifted through my brain.

"I didn't know you smoked."

Laura blew a big cloud of gray upward. "I don't, really. Only after a vigorous workout, like a feisty brawl or a round of raunchy sex."

"Interesting," I noted. "You use 'fight' references for both."

"That's because they can both be rough."

"I hope the fellow in your bed doesn't end up fighting for his breath every time," I told her. "Did you see the way that guy's eyes rolled up into his head?"

She took a sip of coffee and looked at me over her cup. "There is no man in my bed these days," she answered with a sultry smile. "But, you know, when there was, there were times when their eyes rolled into their heads and I had to take their pulses, too."

I shook my head and laughed. I was definitely getting the feeling I was in over my head. This gal was starting to remind me of the black widow spider that killed the male after mating. But what a way to go.

"I'm scaring you!" she exclaimed.

"Who? Me?" I asked, rejecting the suggestion. "You can't be serious."

"I saw you gulp."

"I was drinking coffee."

"No, you weren't, liar. Your cup is empty."

I looked down. She was right.

"I'm a cop," she said. "I notice these things."

"I was, too. And, if anything, it was more of a swallow than a gulp."

"Huh, some cop," she said affably. "I saw the way you fight."

"That's not fair," I responded sheepishly. "The guy suckered me."

Laura finished off her coffee and put the cup down. "Well, I better try to get a cab. I don't want to get busted."

That surprised me. I had forgotten she'd had quite a buzz on just before the altercation with the clowns at the poker table. That whole affair had only been 15 or 20 minutes ago, but she had carried herself pretty well since.

"I'm impressed by the way you hold your liquor," I told her.

She got up slowly, steadied herself with both hands on the table, and looked me in the eye. "I usually hold him by the ears," she said with a slight slur.

"Okay," I announced, standing up and laughing. "I think we better call it a night."

"You were supposed to be my knight," she said with a pout. "Remember?"

"You're right. The knightly thing for me to do would be to give you a lift home."

"It would, but damn, I just remembered I need my car first thing in the morning. I have an appointment I can't miss."

"Well, I could drive you in your car and swing back here in a cab if it's easy enough to find one near your place at this time of night."

Laura thought that funny. "Oh, yeah, you can find one right at my place. I'm staying at the Tropical Towers."

"You live in a hotel?"

"Nah, I'm just lying low for a few days. Don't want to hang around my house and have to deal with some issues."

I thought she might be having boyfriend troubles and I didn't want to intrude.

"Okay," I said brightly. "That's the plan then. I'll drive you to the Towers and take a cab back here."

Laura studied me for a moment. "You'd do that for me?"

"Sure, it's no big deal. I've had a good night: helped out a buddy, had a couple free beers, free food, met you and watched you kick ass . . . and I even got a tax receipt for $180 to boot. What more could a guy ask for?"

Suddenly, she clenched my right wrist in her left hand and twisted my arm into a rather painful position; then she leaned over, kissed me on the cheek, and whispered, "A lot more if he asks nicely."

"Um, okay, but, ouch, that hurts."

"Tsk," she said, easing up the pressure. "Don't be such a baby."

"But that hurt," I explained, rubbing the ligaments.

"Not that much. And haven't you ever heard that controlled pain can be an exquisite extension of pleasure?"

I took her by the elbow, gently, and we began to leave the gymnasium. "You're making this up."

"I am not! Be a good boy and I'll show you sometime."

"You probably mean be a *bad* boy, and you'll show me."

She rested her head on my shoulder as we went through the double doors and down the hall. "That'll work, too."

The parking lot was two-thirds empty and we had no problem finding Laura's car even though she couldn't remember where she had parked. It was a little red Miata, top up, and it was sitting by itself in front of a chain-link fence.

"There she is," Laura cried out. "There's my baby."

When we got near, Laura said hello to the car, explained I'd be driving, and handed me the keys as she walked around to the passenger side.

Okay, I'd met stranger women, but never this attractive and fascinating. One could overlook little things, like their mental aptitude when under the influence, to find out what really made them tick.

I followed Laura and opened her door. Then I scrambled back to my side and got in. It was a tight fit, but eventually I was able to close the door, adjust the mirrors, and get her fired up. The engine, that is. Laura was already fired up enough for both of us, and because of the classic rock she cranked up on the radio, I felt like a teenager again.

I drove with due diligence through the police parking lot, but once we were out on the road, I chirped the tires going from first to second and from second to third just for the hell of it.

"There's never a cop around when you need one," Laura laughed.

"You gonna pull me over?" I asked, as I checked the rear-view.

"If I pull you over, and in this little car, you might not be able to walk for a couple of days, cowboy."

"Yippee-yi-aye," I said with little conviction.

Laura must have sensed something in my tone. "What's wrong?" she asked.

"I'm not sure."

"Christ, Jake. You're more paranoid than I am."

"It's not paranoia," I explained. "It's a force of habit — from my days as a cop, and from the times I leave a card game with a lot of cash on me."

I turned at the next right and watched in the rear-view.

"Shit."

"What is it?"

"A set of headlights pulled out of a parking spot at the curb right after we left. It's still with us."

"Double shit," she said and reached for the key ring stuck in the ignition.

"What are you doing?" I asked.

"I need a key on here," she said, fumbling with the assortment.

I shook my head and made an immediate left down a side street. "There isn't a jealous boyfriend behind all this, is there?"

She looked up at me with no smile. "You wish."

That didn't sound good.

"I was afraid of something like this," she spat.

Laura pried off one of the smaller keys and reached for the glove compartment. It finally flipped open and she pulled out a leather holster with what looked like an M9 Beretta inside it. She unsnapped the catch, held the 9mm stretched out in front, and slapped one into the chamber.

"You weren't shittin' me earlier about being a cop, were you?" she asked.

"I put in almost 10 years. Half of them in Vice."

"Then here," she said, as she pulled something small and pearl white out of the glovebox. "I'm sorry it's all I've got. My big stuff is locked in the trunk."

I took the little pistol. "What the hell is this? Does it work?"

"Of course it works," she said and slammed closed the compartment. "It's an s&w 637."

I examined the petite gun. "I didn't know Smith and Wesson made a .38 this small."

"I use it undercover. Literally." Laura turned her body and looked out the back window. "I usually wear it under a skirt."

I tried to picture that without saying anything that would make her hurt my wrist again.

"Get this baby out where we can use her speed."

I glanced back and the car behind had followed my turn and was now making up the distance in a hurry.

"What the hell!" I exclaimed, and tried to decipher exactly where we were. "Who are these guys? And why are we so worried that we have to pack heat?"

I spun onto the Maryland Parkway without heeding the stop sign and headed south. At this time of the morning traffic was thin with the congestion being reserved for The Strip.

"I'm not a hundred percent sure myself," she said. "But I've got a pretty good idea."

"Yeah, well." I gunned the sports car through an intersection where the lights had just turned red. We made it through to the sounds of blaring horns and angry drivers giving us the bird. "I'm thinking it has something to do with staying at a hotel instead of your house."

"It could."

Tires screeched behind us and then the sound of crushing metal and busting glass erupted. The pursuing vehicle had caused a major crash at the last intersection.

"Damn it!" Laura yelled. "They made it through."

I glanced back and saw the trailing car was gaining.

"Hang on," I said, as I stomped on the brakes and spun the wheel left. We did a 180 and climbed the median facing the opposite direction. As I hit the gas and tried to get off the island, the Miata struck a light standard. The chase car came to a screeching skid, tires smoking, no more than 30 or 40 feet away. Someone in a ski mask pointed what looked like an MP7 out the side window.

"Oh, shit!" I yelled, and fell to my right in an attempt to get below window level.

The sound of my voice was lost as the steady rain of machine gun bullets slammed into the candy apple paint job with a series of thuds. The windows on my side cracked and shattered as shards sprayed chaotically throughout the interior. I heard Laura cry out beside me. The stick shift was beneath me and I tried to negotiate it into reverse blindly.

"You okay?" I shouted.

"Yeah, but get us the hell out of here!"

Laura moved out of her seat and started out her window as the automatic fire ceased for a reload. She sat on the open window ledge with her legs inside and looked out over the roof past my side. I heard her open up with a steady stream from her 9mm, which seemed to keep our assailants hunkered down in their vehicle.

I managed to shove the gearshift down and to the right and I felt the little car jump back from the post. Laura was in a reload herself and I anticipated the return fire from the machine gun at any second. I pointed my little pea shooter out my window and managed to get five shots off at the other car before my gun clicked empty.

The ski mask reappeared and bullets started striking the Miata again.

I grabbed for Laura as I shifted the stick, spun the wheel blindly right, and pressed down on the accelerator.

"Hang on." The car caromed off the light standard as I peeked over the dash. We were well out on the street heading back from where we had started. I pulled myself up, tugged Laura inside, and straightened our course.

"We should be heading for the highway," she suggested as she looked behind us.

"Forget it. We don't know how banged up your little baby is. The tires feel okay, but we can't take any chances." I searched in all directions for a squad car. "If a cop doesn't show up soon, we're going to have to find one ourselves."

"Here come the bad guys," said Laura. "They're about a block behind."

I made it through the intersection with the pileup of innocent cars and considered waiting around for a patrol car. Too dangerous. Instead I floored it back up the parkway.

"Where are we going?" asked Laura.

I looked over at her and saw blood on her face and neck.

"To a hospital soon, by the looks of it. But first we're going back to friendly ground."

I made a few more turns with the chase car still behind. I eventually found what I was looking for and tromped on the gas as we did over 80 down the side street. As we approached our destination, the glare from the headlights behind us diminished as the other vehicle dropped back. I slowed down to about 30, turned into the Police Command facility we had just left 15 minutes ago, and drove right up over the grass and up to the front door. I pressed both palms down on the center of the steering wheel.

Thankfully the horn still worked and the shrill noise brought out the desk sergeant and a bunch of people who appeared to be just leaving. As if on cue, one of the hubcaps came loose and rolled into a juniper bush near the startled onlookers. No cars followed us in.

I took my hands off the horn as I saw Oakley's bulk come through the door with Alexander "The Bull" Bulloch right behind. The lieutenant put his hands on his hips and surveyed the holes down the driver's side, the shattered windows, and the steam rising from the hood; then he poked his head in my window, looked at me, shook his head, and glanced at Laura.

"Well, Laura," he said, as he handed her a handkerchief to wipe her face. "Don't say I didn't warn you about Jake Morgan."

Chapter JACK

"I'll bet my Bugatti this had nothing to do with me," I stated emphatically as I stepped out of the car.

The Bull opened the passenger door. "You okay, Laura?"

"Yeah," she said with a curl of her lip. "You should see the other guys."

He shook his head and snickered. "Same old Laura," he said.

"Anybody need an ambulance?" somebody asked.

Bulloch attentively checked Laura's head. "Looks like some glass nicked her on the forehead," he said with some relief. "Won't be needing any stitches." He wiped gingerly down her neck. "But we'll get them both to the hospital for a look-see."

A crowd had now gathered around the car and speculative whispers circled like a desert dust devil. Oakley sent one of his minions to fetch his car and 30 seconds later up pulled a dark green Crown Victoria.

"What a way to top off the night," announced The Bull, as he opened the front passenger door and guided Laura in. When she was safely tucked inside with her seat belt strapped on, he shut her door, opened the rear door, and pointed for me to get inside.

Oakley took us out of the parking lot and in 15 minutes we were pulling into a reserved for police parking spot at the Emergency entrance of Sunrise Hospital. There was no real reason for me to go for a checkup as I wasn't hurt or leaking any vitals. A helpful nurse took Laura into another room to check for any additional pieces of glass that may have been overlooked under her hair, and to clean up where she had been cut. The three of us guys went to an empty waiting room and Oakley bought us each a cup of nasty, brownish coffee.

When we were settled in, Bulloch said to me, "The lieutenant tells me you were on the force back East."

I nodded.

"Do you have any idea what went down tonight?"

"I know what happened, I just don't know why."

"Give us the whole story as you saw it," The Bull said.

So I did. Everything had occurred so quickly that my recap only took a minute or two.

"And you figured the safest place to get to would be the party at the command facility," said Bulloch. "Smart choice."

"Never a cop around when you need one," I told him.

The Bull ignored that.

"So, Lieutenant Oakley here tells me it was you that heard somebody talking about me earlier tonight. Something about a possible ambush."

"*Overheard*," I pointed out. "I wasn't part of the conversation. As far as I know, the party in question isn't aware I overheard anything."

"Hmm," muttered The Bull; then he looked over at the lieutenant. "Why would anyone care about me if I was retiring? That doesn't make sense."

"Beats me," said Oakley.

Bulloch pondered the situation as he tapped his stir stick on the edge of his Styrofoam cup. "Something's fucked up."

"Like what?"

"Think about it. First, Morgan here stumbles over some of my colleagues who have a hate-on for me and supposedly want to take me out." He chuckled as if at some distant thought. "That wouldn't be the first time I'd heard that, by the way, but, and I'll say it again: why when I'm retiring?

I'm not a threat to anybody while I'm chasing a little white ball around a golf course. Or planting things in my garden."

"Go on," Oakley said.

"Well, second, just after all this retribution bullshit, Laura gets followed and somebody tries to aerate her and her little sports car."

"And me," I offered.

The Bull shook his head. "I don't think they even knew you were in the car. Or cared." Suddenly, Bulloch's head snapped up and his eyes went wide. "Wait a minute. What did these guys say, exactly, when you overheard them?"

"What do you mean? I already told you."

He put his cup down and looked me in the eyes. "Try to remember exactly what they said when they referred to me. Did they say 'The Bull' had to be dealt with?"

I thought back. "I guess. They said 'Bulloch.' So what?"

Now Oakley caught the drift of what The Bull was getting at. "Jesus Christ," he said in a loud whisper.

Bulloch sat back, let out a big breath, and nodded at the lieutenant. "Yup. That has to be it."

I studied the two men and tried to decipher what had just been said by all three of us. I may have been a bit slower, but the sudden realization made my eyes widen also. "Holy shit!" I yelled. "Laura's your niece. She's a Bulloch too. Are you guys saying the hit these guys were talking about was never meant for The Bull?"

"Think about it," said Oakley. "It stands to reason."

I knew my face looked puzzled. "But why would they be talking about Laura?"

Oakley shrugged his shoulders. "Why would they be talking about Alex?"

The Bull sat there, thinking to himself. If he knew, he wasn't saying.

What he did say was "We all know, as cops, that it is easy to step on the wrong toes, especially when you rise up the ladder. There's a lot of political bullshit and phony ass-kissing."

"Been there, done that," I added.

"Well," Oakley continued. "Laura's in a very serious job with some very serious criminal characters. She's more likely to have made enemies on the streets than Alex would in his office job."

Bulloch nodded. "Laura's working with the worst scum in Las Vegas, and that's saying something. So who's to say somebody she busted isn't showing a bit of payback?"

"That MP7 was a little extreme," I said.

"They weren't setting an example," said Oakley. "They wanted her dead. You were just baggage caught in the crossfire."

"And I doubt it had anything to do with bad guys she's put away," I said. "That conversation I overheard, followed up by this trigger-happy car chase, is too much of a coincidence. Face it, guys."

Bulloch looked grave. "Our department is no more lily white than any other," he said. "And there is another possibility . . . that it wasn't outsiders at all, but people in her own squad, people who are against her taking over."

"Taking over?" I asked.

"Yeah," said The Bull. "Laura's on the short list for candidates to take my position when I retire."

Oakley got up and walked to the vending machines. "Anybody for another coffee?"

I looked at him as if he were nuts. "Are you kidding me? I've had enough death threats for one night."

Oakley snickered. "You'd have a tough time being a homicide dick then." He took the hot container and blew over its edge as he walked over to the window. It was still predawn and he stood there looking out into the darkness.

"I'm gonna go have a smoke and check up on Laura." The Bull got up, stretched, and left the room.

Eventually Oakley came out of his reverie at the window and said to no one in particular, "In Homicide, we're trained to look at a case from every possible angle. We try to cover every probable scenario. And, you know, there is one other solution to this whole thing we haven't thought of."

I looked up. "Like what?"

Oakley turned around to face me. "You won't like it."

"Why? None of this has anything to do with me."

"Probably not," said the lieutenant. "But what about Mrs. K.'s murder? As head of the investigative team, I've got a pretty tight lid on things. But what if some details of the case were leaked somehow? What if it became news that you were actually there? If you were the bad guy, wouldn't you want to take care of a possible eye-witness?"

The gist of what Oakley was saying was coming together in my brain.

"I don't want to be an alarmist, or anything," continued the lieutenant, "but what if those shooters you ran into tonight were actually after you?"

Now that was an unpleasant thought I could have done without.

Chapter

Laura and The Bull came out of the examination room just as Oakley dropped his little bomb. She was wearing a bright smile and a small butterfly bandage at the hairline of her left temple.

"Hi, guys."

"I'm glad to see you looking and feeling well," I told her.

"That's Laura," announced Bulloch. "She can still pull off looking good even when she's banged up."

"Oh, Alex, stop it," she pleaded as she playfully punched The Bull on the upper arm. "You're going to scare poor Jake off."

"Nah," said Oakley. "I can vouch for Morgan; he ain't smart enough to know when he's met his match."

"*Tsk tsk,*" Laura contested. "You're getting as bad as my uncle!"

I did have to admit she still looked amazingly provocative, in a dangerous, bewitching way. It reminded me of the first time I saw the white tigers from the Siegfried and Roy show in their natural habitat at the entrance to the Mirage hotel: wonderful to watch and marvel at, but savage and frantic.

We sat around and watched Oakley drink another cup of murky coffee while Laura and I went over the details of the night. The two cops listened intently and appeared genuinely concerned.

It was almost 4 a.m. when we left the hospital. A lot of the bars, restaurants, and shops had closed for a few hours and dimmed their neon. The lieutenant dropped Laura off at the Trop Towers and Bulloch said he wanted to have a few more words with his niece and to make sure she got to her room safely.

Before she left, Laura leaned in through my window, gave me a kiss on the cheek, and thanked me for being there through the car-chase ordeal. I wanted to thank her for saving my ass at the poker table, but I knew I wouldn't hear the end of it from Oakley. As she started to leave, Laura opened her purse and handed me a white business card. She gave me a sultry smile and told me to use the cell number if I decided I could handle the ride.

On the way back to pick up the Bugatti, Oakley asked me if I had a few minutes to stop at the Police Information and Data Gathering Depot.

"You mean the donut shop?"

"Yeah."

"Sure, why not? It has to be better than that hospital swill." I glanced at my watch: 4:22. "And if we're lucky, the apple fritters will be fresh out of the oven."

Oakley smiled his concurrence. "Once a cop. . . ."

We sat in the car and slurped real coffee while we munched freshly baked goods and watched other unmarked and official cars drop in. A few cops recognized Oakley and came over to say hello. Everyone took note of me, but nobody paid real attention. That was okay with me; I had a lot going through my mind.

Between visits, Oakley and I discussed the whys and wherefores of what had happened tonight. Or last night — as the sun had now begun to break over the aptly named Sunrise mountain range.

"Well," Oakley said. "It looks like the conversation you overheard in the locker room must have had something to do with Laura, not The Bull."

"Seems that way to me," I agreed.

Oakley appeared as solemn as I'd ever seen him — and in the last year I'd seen him as he stood over a number of dead bodies. He shook his head in a sad fashion and sighed. "I don't like the implications," he finally said.

"How so?"

"I may be Homicide, but the Vice guys are still brothers. All of our badges say 'Clark County.' If what we're thinking is true, it's going to reflect on the entire force."

"Yeah, but don't kid yourself. There isn't a major city in the nation that can claim a perfectly clean police force," I insisted. "We had problems back in Boston, where a couple of senior officers were getting kickbacks from tow truck companies and body shops. One of them, a captain no less, had his mortgage paid off as a part of his package. The other had three kids put through college. When word leaked, all hell broke loose. Now they had another four guys who wanted to be fed from the trough in similar fashion.

"They demanded a piece of the pie. And they didn't threaten to go to Internal Affairs. They threatened the original officers and a couple of the 'bakers' who were supplying all the pie."

"Ouch. Not a good thing."

"Nope. There was a lot of money involved and they were dealing with the wrong crowd. Two of the four were found in a car, two bullets in each of their brains. The third one they found scattered over his front lawn and driveway shortly after he started his car."

Oakley waited a moment and then asked, "What about the fourth?"

I chewed thoughtfully, and washed down the last of my donut. "Well, he was the one least involved in the whole thing, a fringe player who thought he'd tripped over the pot at the end of the rainbow."

Just to wrap up the story, I was going to tell the lieutenant that the guy had got whacked and leave it at that, but there were too many things popping up here that reminded me of what had gone down back East.

"This last guy was in a whole lot of trouble from a couple of other things he was involved in: heavy gambling, way over his head in debt, stealing confiscated criminal goods and cash from the police property room to cover his losses until he could pay it back."

"Jesus."

"And right when this was all going down, he goes and gets himself involved in two separate fatalities: a shooting and a knifing. The cops found out about a lot of what was going on and, to save face and keep it all out of the press, they honorably discharged the guy."

"Poor bastards," sighed Oakley. "They just never learn."

"Some of them do."

The sun was now fully over Sunrise and heading for the edge of the Frenchman's range.

"So what happened to the guy?" the lieutenant asked. "Where'd he end up?"

I rolled up the napkin and flicked a bunch of crumbs off my chest.

"Vegas."

"Vegas?" asked Oakley incredulously. "What the hell's he doing here?"

I tossed the crumpled bag out my window and watched it hit the rim of the waste receptacle and fall to the asphalt parking lot.

"He's sitting in an unmarked police car at a donut shop spilling out his life story to some cop named Oakley."

Chapter

"Seriously, Morgan. Are you shittin' me?"

"I wish I was."

He sat there looking at me like a father who'd just learned his son liked to wear frilly girls' clothes and lots of makeup.

"Jesus H. Christ!" His shout was filled with exasperation. "You've told me a lot of bad things about your past since I've known you, but. . . ." He had difficulty as he tried to put the words together. "Are you tellin' me you were a dirty cop?"

"I was in bad shape," I said softly. "My world was totally upside down from the gambling situation I'd got myself into, and I knew it was probably just a matter of time before it all blew up in my face. But you know diehard gamblers."

"Yeah. Met a few."

"We always keep thinking we'll hit that one big score that will sort everything else out."

"Sure, the old Vegas adage: *'Please God, let me get even and I'll never play again.'*"

"Yeah," I managed to chuckle. "That's the one."

"You told me once about the big game where you had just got yourself even, and then the place got robbed. That's where the kid got shot. So he was one of the fatals you were just talking about?"

I nodded.

"Go on."

"Well, it was just before that when I lost my partner."

"You've mentioned that, too. She was the one you were going to move in with, but then she was killed during some informant meet." Oakley nodded his head. "Yeah, now it's all coming back to me. You were both supposed to be there. And you might have been able to save her if you'd been able to get your compulsive ass out of the card game you were stuck in."

"I missed her by eight or nine minutes . . . a couple of hands."

The lieutenant shook his head and looked disgusted. "So what did all that have to do with the shakedown your buddies had planned?"

"The thing is we weren't even buddies. They were just three guys in my unit. I was the one who learned about the little vehicle scam that the higher-ups had going. The three of them hatched the plan and were going to cut me in on it for passing the info on to them."

"But then the proverbial shit hit the fan."

"Yeah."

"You know," said Oakley in an amazed tone. "It's a weird coincidence that you're on the edge of something similar happening here."

"It dawned on me," I admitted. "That's why I just told you what I did."

"You never cease to amaze me, Morgan. You get yourself neck-deep in so much shit and come out smelling like roses."

"Attractive simile."

"Don't be a smartass," Oakley said sternly. "It's bad enough you're involved in the robbery and death of Mrs. Kobayashi; I do *not* want you getting involved in something that may be coming down within Metro here in Vegas. Understand?"

"I'm already involved and you know it. That happened when they took their first shot at me."

"Nothing's happened so far that can't have your involvement cleverly erased — including you meeting Laura Bulloch."

"But that's the reason why I have to stay on this, if only to watch Laura's back."

"Why is that?" asked Oakley incredulously.

I took in and let out a lungful of air. "I have to do this, or at least do what I can."

"This isn't your fight, Morgan."

"In a way that maybe only I understand, it is."

"The hell with you, then," Oakley yelled. "I'll lock you up on some trumped-up charges to do with the Kobayashi case and keep you on ice until this thing is settled."

"But I have to help, Oak," I pleaded.

"What are you talking about, Morgan?"

"My partner, back in Boston?"

"Yeah?"

"I don't think her dying had anything to do with a CI meet that went wrong."

"But you told me she was meeting a confidential informant. You were both supposed to."

"That's the thing," I explained. "The CI, when we caught up with him, had an air-tight alibi. He was at a meeting with his parole officer when it happened."

I could see the confusion on Oakley's face.

"So," I went on, "the way I pieced it together later, it was a set-up from the get-go. I was supposed to be taken out by the same guys who took out my buddies."

"Shit," said Oakley softly. "They got your girlfriend and missed you."

"And that's why I have to be involved here."

The lieutenant caught on. "Redemption."

"Something like that."

"Shit," he said again. He got out of the car, slammed the door, and went into the donut shop. A minute later he came out with two more coffees.

"You know," he said, when he got comfortable again behind the wheel. "I know you're attracted to Laura, but you're just going to be in the way."

"How will I be in the way?" I asked. "I'm going to be behind the scenes, watch her back."

Oakley thought some more. "She's an exemplary officer. Been doing an outstanding job in Vice for over seven years. If she wasn't being considered for captain of the Vice Division, I'd try to get her into Homicide. I think that much of her. There aren't enough strong females on our staff and we could use her."

"I know what you mean," I deadpanned. "Shows like csi have good-looking females on them. Must put a lot of pressure on you and your department."

"That's got nothing to do with it, but it doesn't hurt politically."

"I guess if she can handle the rigors of Vice, she should be able to deal with Homicide."

"She's as smart as she is tough, Morgan. Don't underestimate her."

"I haven't. I just want to help make sure she doesn't get hurt."

"Yeah, I saw how well you saved her from those guys at the poker table."

"That's not fair. I got suckered!"

Oakley managed a smile. "I think highly of Laura. If I can't persuade you to stay out of it altogether, then just make sure you remember you aren't a cop anymore. If you want to hang around with her and keep her company, who knows, maybe that'll be enough to keep them away until the department gets a line on them. If it's cops though, then they're going to know you're no threat."

"Or they won't give a shit."

"There's that, too."

We sat there for a minute, sipping, and then Oakley said, "Do what you have to do. I'll never admit to it in a court of law, but in a crazy, messed-up way, I might start to respect what you're doing. You've shown me you can handle yourself in the past, so I know you're not a total slouch, but don't go thinking you're Metro. And for Christ's sake, don't go shooting anybody. Laura already told us about the pea shooter you fired off when you helped her out in the Miata. But don't go cowboy on me and pick up your own piece. That's zero tolerance around here. You'll be hung out to dry and I won't be able to do anything about it."

"That's okay. I'm not crazy about guns in the first place."

"Good. So it's settled. If Laura wants you around, you'll be there to back her up. I know The Bull has already offered her protection in a safe house until this blows over, but she just laughed it off. And for some unknown reason she seems to like you, so maybe you'll be of some use. But if you ask me, I think she's going to use you, abuse you, and then spit you out in little pieces."

I couldn't help but match his smile. "I appreciate your concern."

"Off the record, I appreciate what you're doing." Oakley turned the ignition and the Ford fired up. "And if you can help sort this out without getting any cops killed, Morgan, I'll owe you one."

"What about if I get killed?" I exclaimed.

Oakley pulled out of the parking lot and appeared to be deep in thought as he drove.

Finally, he asked, "Can you write me in your will for the Bugatti? I love that car."

Chapter

I slept until mid-afternoon and woke up only because of the dream I was having. It took place in the days of King Arthur and I was a prince who had just saved the damsel Laura from the evil sheriff. She'd shown her appreciation by stealing my steed and shoving me off a cliff. As I was pondering what it could have meant, the phone rang.

"Hey, sleepyhead. It's me."

"Hey," I said back to her. "I was just dreaming about you."

"Really?" she said in a pleased tone. "I'm flattered."

I wiped sleep from my eyes. "You stole my horse," I told her.

There was a long pause at the other end.

"You okay, Jake? That punch you took last night, you didn't get a concussion now, did you?"

"No," I answered, in between a long, loud yawn. "Never mind. It's a long story."

"Well, get your ass out of bed," she ordered. "I've got some things to do. A bit of shopping, this and that. Then we can get something to eat."

"Uh, yeah, I guess. . . ."

"Meet me in an hour."

I tried to remember if I had anything already planned for today. "Yeah, sure. At the Trop?"

"No, I'll be out."

She gave me an address way out on West Charleston Boulevard, an area of the city popular with the local suburbanites, but one that I wasn't too familiar with.

"How'd you get my number," I asked as I remembered I hadn't given it to her.

"Did you forget?" she asked. "I'm a cop."

An hour later I was standing in a small strip mall of 10 stores and looking around for Laura or a damsel in distress. A number of women with children in strollers walked by nervously, looking at me as if I might swoop away their prodigies. I couldn't help but wonder why I was having such a weird impression on people. I'd combed my hair and checked my zipper twice. I waited around for about 10 minutes, when suddenly the door of the store I was standing in front of opened and out stepped Laura.

"There you are," she called out brightly.

"Hi. I was looking for you out in the parking lot. You've been inside shopping all this time?"

"I haven't shopped yet. I was just paying off my account."

I glanced up at the sign over my head.

DOM 'N OH OH OHS! In small print beneath it read *Love until it hurts.* . . .

I looked at the window where a large color poster of Ilsa, head of the supposed female Nazi division, was taped to the glass inside. The character was scantily dressed in erotic S&M leather military fatigues and brandished a black crop with tassels. A male prisoner in a tattered uniform bowed at her feet. The bold caption *"You will do as I say, you male dog!"* shouted out to anyone on the sidewalk from right beside where I had stood when the soccer moms walked by with their little urchins.

I shook my head. "No wonder I was making such an impression with the people out here."

"Don't be such a fuddy-duddy," said Laura. "Come on inside and help me with my shopping." She held the door for me.

"I don't know about this," I told her apprehensively.

"Hurry up," she whispered hoarsely as she looked up and down the sidewalk in a mocking manner. "I don't want the kiddies to hear any of the screaming coming from inside."

"Very funny," I told her and stepped through the door.

Nobody screamed.

♦

I followed Laura down the first wall of accessories. An extensive array of leather attire and knee-high boots caught her attention first. She flipped through the clothes like I used to with my baseball card collection.

"Got it, got it, need it, got it," she rattled off as she walked down the aisle.

I studied her as she moved, and my imagination ran rampant as I pictured what she might look like in some of the outfits. My reverie was broken when a voice called out.

"Can I help you, sir?"

A goth salesgirl, complete with dyed, ultra ebony hair, black lipstick, and three or four rings in different parts of her face, looked at me with a knowing smile.

"I'm sorry," I apologized. "I must have been daydreaming."

"I could see," she told me, pleased. "Mistress B is one of our best customers."

When she said the word "best," her tongue piercing clicked against one of her front teeth.

"Are you a newbie?" she asked with interest.

"Apparently not for long."

"Can I interest you in anything?" asked the eager salesgirl. "We're having a sale on penile apparatus."

"Uh, no, not right now," I said as I spotted Laura hoisting an enormous double-headed rubber dildo and waving it back and forth at me. "Excuse me. I think Ms. B is being attacked by a giant anaconda."

I left the bemused clerk and hurried over to Laura, who had put back the two-way toy and now had a cat-o'-nine-tails in her hands.

"Turn around and bend over for a sec, Jake," she said.

I took the whip from her and placed it back in its rack. "What are we doing here?"

She looked at me and smiled saucily. "Stocking up," she said. "I feel a marathon coming on."

"Oh, really?" I laughed nervously as I picked up a pair of handcuffs. "And who's the poor victim, um, I mean who's the lucky man?"

"Looks like you're it," Laura said and laughed. She took the manacles from me. "I found those are too easy for guys to escape from. I use my working cuffs."

"Interesting," I said.

I reminded myself to look for the set of universal police keys with which I had absconded when I left the force. I'd known they might come in handy someday, but I had never pictured the scenario that ran through my head now.

"And kinky," I added.

"Oh, yeah." She took my hand and we walked deeper into the store.

Still no screams.

We spent the next half-hour browsing through playthings that wouldn't be carried by Toys 'R' Us. I was introduced to bondage belts, restraints, muzzles, collars, and ball gag head harnesses. Next were electrodes, floggers, stingers, whips, ticklers, and something called "the deluxe samurai male chastity cage complete with thigh separators," at which point I was going to draw the line and leave — Laura, or no Laura.

The final decision came immediately after I was shown the Pet Play exhibit, which featured a naked guy wearing an inserted rubber puppy tail.

As I made a beeline for the front door, I heard Laura call out, "Bad doggie."

Chapter

"Nice wheels."

We were motoring down Rainbow Boulevard gathering attention and stares. Some of the kids waved as we went by and a lot of their fathers nodded their admiration. I wasn't sure if it was directed at the car or Laura. In the back seat were two large bags filled with new toys that Laura had not let me see.

"What kind of Buggy did you say it was?"

"It's a Bugatti," I corrected, and spelled it out for her. "A model T57. Italian. It was one of the last ones off the assembly line before wwii in 1939."

As impressed as she seemed to be with the car, a frown formed.

"What's wrong?" I asked.

"Nothing really," she said. "It's just not the kind of car I picture you driving."

"Sorry. My '79 Chevy Vega fell apart. Died on me."

She made a face. "Eww."

"The Bugatti was a gift. A reward, really. For a job I did for a family last fall."

"Some reward."

"Yeah, well, it was some family."

I wasn't about to get into the Bonello family and their ties to a certain large, furtive, ethnic organization — especially not to a vice cop. At least not without a good whipping from a cat-o'-nine-tails.

I had been following Laura's directions and in a few minutes we pulled into the parking lot of Michael's Steak House. It was a high-end restaurant that I had heard about but never been able to afford. As we walked in, I wondered how I was going to afford it now.

A pleasant maître d' greeted us as if we were old friends and escorted us to a dark, romantic table in the far corner. A gray-haired gentleman sporting a handlebar mustache wandered the room playing dulcet tones from a violin that looked like it had been placed under his chin at birth.

We had barely studied the leather-bound menu when a handsome, dark-haired fellow in an impeccable black suit appeared at our table. I wasn't a cop any longer, but I deduced that this was probably Michael.

"Laura," he said, with a hint of an Italian accent as he took her hand in both of his. "How wonderful to see you again."

They exchanged pleasantries for a few moments, and at one point he glanced at me, over at Laura, and then back to me. His look and smile read *Oh, boy, you don't know what you're in for, you poor bugger.*

"Michael, I'd like to introduce you to my new friend, Jake."

He gave me a curt nod, bowed slightly, and extended a hand. "Officer."

Michael turned his attention back to Laura. "If I may, I recommend the rib-eye tonight." He leaned over and said in a hushed tone, "I have a few that were aged an extra two weeks and put aside for my most special customers."

A smiling waiter arrived at our table and Michael excused himself by telling Laura to ask for him if she needed anything. He gave me a big wink and left.

"Do you get that often?" Laura asked after she had sent the waiter off in search of a bottle of her favorite red wine and I nonchalantly glanced at the wine list.

"Lots of guys get winked at by other guys."

"No, silly," she said. "The cop thing. He called you 'Officer.'"

"Yeah, a fair bit," I answered, as I finally found the price of the bottle. "Ouch."

"Oh, come on," she said light-heartedly. "There are worse things to look like."

"I guess."

The two of us made smalltalk as we surveyed the menus. I tried to determine if I had enough cash on me, not only for the meal, but for the $89 jug of vino she'd just ordered. To make matters worse, I was pretty sure the one credit card I owned was maxed at its $500 limit, and I hadn't made a payment in two or three months. Although I doubted Michael took Home Depot, I remembered I might have a few emergency casino chips in the car that I hadn't cashed in.

The waiter returned with a triumphant look on his face. "You're both in luck," he beamed. "Our last bottle. I searched high and low and found it in the wine cellar."

"How fortunate for us, Jake."

"Yes, lucky you and me." If I was *really* blessed, the guy would have tripped on the stairs and dropped the bottle. Mogen David would have been fine for me.

The waiter didn't even bother to ask if I wanted to test-taste the wine. Instead he stood beside Laura, popped the cork, and announced he would take our order as he allowed the wine to breathe. How considerate.

Laura mentioned Michael's recommendation and the waiter said, "That is an excellent choice, madam, but may I be so bold as to ask if you are extra hungry?"

"I'm famished," she told him. "Haven't eaten all day."

Which reminded me that I hadn't either.

She looked at me over the top of her menu and said, "And I think I may need my strength tonight."

"Wonderful," replied the waiter. "In that case, may I suggest you go for the 14 ounce rather than the 10? They are identically aged, but the marbling is outstanding in the 14."

It was starting to sound like a fashion show.

Laura was ecstatic. "That's terrific. What do you say, Jake? Do you want to slap a big one on?"

No, but I wanted to slap our helpful waiter. He was measuring the difference as four ounces, while I was measuring it at the difference between $32.95 and $49.95. The little bastard's gratuity was quickly dwindling down to spare change.

I squished up my face.

"You know," I told them, "I had a huge lunch this afternoon." For effect, I patted my paunch. "And I'm trying to watch my waistline." I proceeded to close my menu with great fanfare and announced, "I think I'll just have a salad."

The waiter seemed to shake his head as he wrote this down on his pad. I noticed Laura as she studied me, obviously having detected something amiss. She had twigged on to me and was trying to decipher the situation. When the waiter had finished jotting down the order, he poured a sample of the wine into Laura's glass and waited patiently for her approval. She swirled it, held it to her nose for a sniff, and sipped a taste. I crossed my fingers and waited for her to spit it out and denounce it as a bad batch of grapes, but instead she nodded and we watched as he filled both our glasses.

"You know," she pronounced slowly to the waiter as she kept her eyes on me. "I'm really, really hungry. Make the 14 a size 18."

"Are you sure they make one that big?" I asked in shock.

"Yes, dear, it's right there under the 14-ouncer." She pursed her lips and said, "Right where it says '$69.95.'" She seemed to be enjoying herself.

"Ah, yes," I replied. "Now I see it."

I closed the menu and handed it to the waiter. He hurried off in search of half a cow.

"The lady has a healthy appetite," I said as I toasted her with my glass. She clinked hers against mine.

"You ain't seen nothin' yet," she warned me.

Chapter

I was grateful when the waiter arrived with a basket of fresh rolls as I knew a measly salad wasn't going to satisfy my appetite.

"So tell me a bit about Jake Morgan," Laura asked.

We sipped our wine and I told her about growing up back East, where I went to Boston U, tried my hand at a few trades, and eventually wound up on the Beantown PD for almost 10 years. She wanted to know why I'd left and I told her how I ended up with a bad case of authority anxiety and political bullshit-itis.

I left out that my partner had been killed and that I had a gambling problem. I figured she'd probably work out the latter for herself soon enough. I fast-forwarded to my arrival in Vegas three and a half years ago, how I went to dealer school, and how I started as a blackjack dealer at the Oasis and ultimately in the poker room.

By the time I was on my fifth bun, the conversation had turned to Laura. I learned that she was a true Vegan, born and bred. Her father had been a cop along with his brother, the infamous Bull, and her mother had been a dispatcher for Metro. Both parents were gone, victims of a horrific airplane accident. The Cessna they were flying went down in the mountains on a trip to Lake Tahoe. Laura had done a stint in nursing when she got out of college, but when her parents died, caved in and joined the force. Her uncle, Alex, had guided her through her career, starting in Traffic and finally into Vice, where she had been for the last seven years.

Our meals arrived and I hadn't felt as depressed in a long time.

"Your Black Angus platter, madam," the waiter announced with a flourish.

I thought about yanking the tablecloth so her side would end up in front of me.

"I apologize for the steak hanging over the edge of your dinnerware," he said almost giddily. "But it was the biggest plate I could find."

"It looks wonderful," observed Laura. "Don't you think so Jake?"

"Uh-huh. . . ." I brought my napkin to my lips in case I started to drool. The waiter finished admiring his work and stepped toward me.

"Oh, yeah," he said, almost as an afterthought. He placed a bowl of assorted lettuces in front of me and wrinkled his nose. "Your greens."

I felt like flattening his nose. Instead I grabbed the last roll and told him to bring another basket.

"Yes," said Laura with a smile, as she cut into her slab of beef. "I wouldn't mind trying one of those buns myself before they run out."

"Sorry," I apologized. "It's this carb thing I have." I dug into my salad. "Mmm."

After a few minutes of watching Laura's eyes seemingly roll back into her head on each bite of steak, I decided it was time to broach the events of last night.

"So what can you tell me about last night?" I asked her.

"Which part?"

"How about the part where we were shot at with a machine gun and almost killed?"

"Ah, that one. What do you want to know? We were driving, somebody was pissed at something or other, and decided to take some shots at us."

I put my fork down. "Look, Laura. I feel some kind of connection to you, for whatever weird reason. But if I'm going to get involved, we're going to have one major understanding. Let's not bullshit one another."

She chewed thoughtfully. "Okay."

"Good," I said. "Now what do you know about these shooters? I know you told your uncle Alex a lot more after we parted last night than you told me."

"And I imagine you and Lieutenant Oakley probably talked after we left you, too."

"We did."

She popped another cube of meat into her mouth. "I've got some problems with some of the people I'm working with."

"Guys in Vice?"

She nodded. "It's a long story. I'm not sure how much I want you to know."

I told her about my overheard conversation in the locker room the previous night.

"Shit," she spat. "Then it's on."

I could figure out what that meant but not why. "Tell me about it."

Laura wiped at her mouth and took a break from her steak, which I noticed wasn't even half finished.

"I don't know you that well, yet. I'll tell you what I think you need to know."

"Go for it."

"There's graft going on in our department. Has been for years. Unfortunately, I came upon it."

I hoped my face didn't give away how close to home this sounded. "And did you go along for the ride?"

"Well, you know what Vice is like, Jake. You get the odd freebie here and there."

"But we're not talking coffee and donuts, are we?"

She cut into her steak again. "No. The problem is that it is much bigger."

"They're false-reporting the amounts in drug hauls?"

Laura nodded.

"Swiping the cash lying around too?"

"Uh-huh." She gave me a quizzical look. "It sounds like you know what I'm talking about."

"Yeah. Been there, done that," I told her.

"But it's getting out of hand," she continued. "They're getting greedy. And they want to call all the shots. They're giving me just enough to shut me up."

"So, you want out?"

Laura laughed. "You don't just 'get out.' And there's too much money involved here, so people are getting very worried. They don't want to spend time in the same jail as some of the guys they put away. That would be very bad for their health."

"You think they would get this extreme?"

"Are you kidding? Some of these guys are tripling their salaries. There's too much at stake."

There was something missing here, but I couldn't put my finger on it.

"Was this the first time they tried anything? Does this have anything to do with you staying at the Trop Towers instead of your house?"

"It's been going on for about a month and a half. I've had a couple of run-ins at my place. Rocks through windows. Tires slashed. Vandalism. I even found my place broken into and tossed. Nothing missing that I could see. But it still scared the hell out of me."

My mind was working overtime and I think she sensed it.

"To tell you the truth, Jake, ever since my hat was thrown in for my uncle's job, it's been escalating. Last night, obviously, was the apex."

"That's what's got me thinking," I said, starting up on my salad again.

"What?"

"I'm wondering if they're setting you up."

"All I know is they don't want me in charge. The Bull might not be aware of the extent of the theft and extortion, but I am. If I win the position, they know the golden goose will get spayed. The golf memberships, the gambling, the boats out on Lake Mead — all gone."

"That's a scenario that plays. But what if they're making it look like you're having trouble with someone, so if anything serious happens to you, it won't look like it's coming from left field. There will have been a pattern and it might deflect any investigation within your department."

She didn't say anything; I had either scared her or touched a nerve. She was still going at the first half of meat on her plate but with little interest.

I had finished my pathetically inadequate meal and couldn't bear to sit there and watch her. I excused myself to go to the bathroom.

In reality, I sneaked out the front door and ran to the Bugatti. I got inside and started to search through the glove compartment for leftover casino chips which might help boost my bankroll high enough to pay for this meal. I whooped aloud as I found three green $25 chips, two from the Palace Station and one from the Palms. If I put them with the hundred or so I had on me, I should just make the bill.

I might have to mail a tip in to the waiter though.

Chapter

I jogged back to the restaurant and quietly walked back to the dining room. The hallway had sections of latticed wood with plants here and there, and as I walked along I could see Michael standing at our table. I stopped for a moment when I saw him reach into his inside jacket pocket and pull out a white envelope, which he proceeded to hand over to Laura. She didn't bother to open it or look inside. Instead she just tucked it into her purse, which hung on her chair. They exchanged a few more words and then he left.

When I took my seat I enviously noted the remainder of her steak was still on her plate. Before I could continue our conversation, Laura looked me in the eye and said, "You know how we made that pact about not bull-shitting each other?"

"Yeah, sure."

"Well, I want to know why you were bullshitting me earlier."

"What are you talking about?"

She gave me a knowing smile. "About having had a big lunch this afternoon."

"What do you mean?"

She laughed out loud. "Are you serious? Jake, you've been eyeing my dinner since it hit the table."

I picked at some crumbs on the tablecloth with my nail. "Well. . . ."

"And the rolls! You ate about a loaf and a half of bread, for God's sake.

You couldn't have been more obvious. Why order just a salad?"

"It's like this," I said sheepishly, and went on to tell her the story of how I didn't think I'd have enough to cover the bill.

She held her napkin to her face and laughed into it until her eyes watered. I sat there running my finger around the edge of my water glass as I waited for her to calm down.

"You are so hilarious, Jake," she finally said, holding her stomach. "I knew it had to be something like that. I could see it in your face when I ordered the wine. And when the waiter talked me up to the 14-ounce steak!"

"Well, I didn't want to look like a shmuck," I explained. "I didn't know we were going to such a posh place."

She dabbed at her eyes, which were still damp. "But you know what's really funny?"

"What's that?"

"I don't get a bill when I come here. Michael and I go way back. It was all on the house!"

I looked at my empty salad bowl and my stomach growled at me angrily. "You mean. . . . ?"

Laura started up again for a brief moment. "Yes!" she cried.

For a second I didn't know if I should laugh or cry. "Sheesh," was all I could think to say.

"Here," she said, pushing over her platter that was only half finished.

My eyes widened and my mouth began to salivate. "You mean it?"

"Of course. Why do you think I changed my mind and went for the gut buster? I knew what you were doing all along. I was just busting your balls."

"You're a very funny gal," I said facetiously. "But man does not live by rolls alone, you know. Now hand me your damn steak knife so I can get at this sucker."

I didn't say anything for the next few minutes and I don't know if Laura did either as I wasn't listening. Cut, chew, and swallow were the only things on my mind.

Laura made a bridge with her fingers and rested her chin on it as she watched me. When I finally pushed the empty plate away, she smiled and said, "And you're a funny guy."

I was feeling much better now and I gave her my best caveman impression: "Yes, me funny. Ha, ha."

She still had her head resting on her fingers, but there was now an obvious twinkle in her eye. "Can I ask you a serious question?"

"Yeah, sure," I said. "Fire away."

"When's the last time you got laid?"

Now that caught me by surprise. "Excuse me?"

She gave me a saucy smile. "You heard me. And I mean *really* laid. You know, the old eye-popping, toe-curling, three stooges 'whoop-whoop-whooping' kinda laid."

"You mean the kind where the only reason you would throw the woman out of bed was so you could screw her again on the floor?"

She nodded. "That's it."

"Well," I paused and thought about it. "I would have to say, uh . . . never?"

The look she gave me was lustful and I knew more than my stamina was going to be road-tested.

"In that case," I replied to her gaze, "I'm all yours, Laura."

"But remember," her face turned serious, "once you're shackled and oiled down, you will address me as Mistress, Mistress Laura, or Mistress of the Dark."

"I like that," I chuckled. "You're filled with surprises. This sounds like it could be fun."

"If you like surprises," she said seductively, "you're in for the ride of your life."

She got up from the table.

"You will follow Mistress Laura and do as you are told."

"This is great," I said with a laugh as I slid out of my seat. "The only thing missing is a leash."

Laura turned and opened her large purse. Inside was a studded collar and leather lead. "Now, heel."

As she turned and started to walk, I answered her in the only way that seemed to make any sense.

"Woof."

Chapter

I went to McClusky before my swing shift on Monday and asked him for a favor. He seemed sympathetic to my request for a low-pressure, low-limit game to deal.

"Jesus Christ," he said, when he saw me. "You look like shit warmed over."

I had no idea what that meant, but that was true of a lot of what could come out of McClusky's mouth, so I usually just agreed with him. This time I did, however, know what he was referring to.

My eyes were bloodshot, the black bags beneath them were more like suitcases, and I was groggier than I had ever felt in my life. Every once in a while, little tics on my face and spasms on my limbs would occur without warning as a result of the electro shocks. Parts of me were sore, some were almost raw, and some were still sensitive from where I had participated in one of Laura's favorite experiments: hot candle wax.

Actually, I didn't have much say at the time as I was either having too much damn fun or was oblivious for some unknown reason. At one point, I wondered if she had spiked my drink with a roofie, or maybe even Viagra. My little marathon had gone on for almost five hours, and for a guy who had gotten laid only twice in the last year, I had now tripled my record with another four.

"You must have taken the passing of poor Mrs. K. worse than I thought," said McClusky.

"I've had a hard time sleeping," I admitted. "I doubt I got two solid hours last night."

"Well, I'm glad you made it in. With it being a holiday Monday and all, we're a little short-staffed." He looked at me with admiration. "But you've always been an ace of mine. You always make it in and you rarely, if ever, screw up. Let me know how you're holding up later, and maybe I can give you a short shift if somebody calls in and wants some hours." He laughed at that. "There's enough of you guys shooting your paychecks that there's usually somebody who'll come in."

"Yeah, well, I've been there, too."

McClusky strained his thick body to the side and pointed at me. "What'd you do to your neck? It looks all scratched up."

"Oh, that," I said, lifting the collar of my shirt a little higher. "Cut myself shaving."

He raised an eyebrow. "What did you shave with? A rose bush?"

"Dull blade," I explained, and tried to change the subject. "So, did Mr. Kobayashi show up?"

He sat back in his chair and sighed. "Yeah, poor bastard. He took it pretty hard. I hear he has his U.S. attorneys talking to Contini's fleet of vultures. Big Julie's afraid they're going to try to sue the hotel for lack of security." He shook his head. "Probably trying to make up for the half a mil he lost in his wife's jewelry."

"Wonder if he misses the money more than his wife?" I mused.

McClusky shrugged. "Dunno. But he dropped a coupla mil over the last few days."

"I'm surprised he felt like shooting so soon."

"Ah, you know these guys. They're sick. Not much stands in their way when they feel the urge to splurge."

"I guess," I said, as I looked at my watch. I gently lifted my body from the chair and winced as I did. "By the way, you haven't said anything to anyone about me being up in the suite when all this shit went down, right?"

McClusky waved a big paw. "Nah, that cop, Oaktree, he came by right after. I think the only ones who know you were there are you, me, and maybe Contini." He rubbed at his five o'clock shadow with his index finger. "You think they're afraid you could get whacked by the gunman if it gets out you might be a witness? The cop said only two, maybe three of them are in on it." It seemed like a bolt of lightning hit him in the ass. "Hey! I was just thinkin'. How come you weren't shot if you were there?"

"Oh, that," I told him. "The robber thought she was alone. He didn't know I was in the can at the time."

"Lucky you."

"Well, Oakley doesn't want to take any chances about the killer knowing I was there," I said. "And to tell you the truth, I'd just as soon nobody else knew either."

McClusky pulled his hulk out of the chair to join me. "No problem, ace. I don't want to see anybody pop you off when we're short-staffed."

He wrapped a thick arm around me and patted me hard enough on the shoulder to make me wince. As uncomfortable as it felt, I guess it could have been worse. If he had pinched my nipples instead, I would have been in real trouble; they were still tender from the alligator clips I was forced to wear earlier that morning. Then again, I suppose if my boss went around squeezing my tits, I'd have a whole different kind of problem to worry about.

♥

I spent a few hours dealing a $1–$3 Hold 'Em game to a bunch of tourists who were looking to learn the game cheaply. It couldn't have been any better for me; I didn't have to think much, I wasn't forced to pay a whole lot of attention, and if I made the odd mistake, there was a good chance nobody would realize it anyway. I could have dealt this game in my sleep.

To my surprise, Lieutenant Oakley, dressed in casual slacks and a beige Desert Inn golf shirt, pulled back a chair at one point and sat in. He nodded hello and I smiled back.

"Didn't know you played," I said.

He pulled out three $10 bills and put them on the table. "I don't."

An old-timer beside him, who I knew to be the only professional player on the table, gave him a warm welcome. "Well, join the rest of us fishes. We're just having a good time."

I took Oakley's money, laid it on the table with the serial numbers face up for the camera, and gave him a stack and a half of white one dollar chips.

"Fishes?" asked the lieutenant.

"Yeah," said the pro. "You know, somebody gets a good hand against you, and then he reels you in!"

A few of the others laughed and one said, "Don't let the old guy fool you. He's reeled in all of us — a couple of hands each."

"Ah, come on," he said in his defense, and winked at me. "I just got lucky."

"So, do you know how the game is played?" I asked Oakley as I started to deal the cards.

"Sure," he said. "I've watched it on television lots of times."

The old man's eyes lit up. "I raise," he said, from the under the gun position.

The following player re-raised and the next one said, "Once more." The old lady sitting beside Oakley said, "Let's cap it."

The lieutenant squeezed his cards apart. "How much to me?"

"It's four dollars to call," I announced, hoping he would just fold and get out of this one for his own good.

He thought about it for a moment and then said, "Well, like they say on TV, the pot's too big." He tossed four white chips in.

Everybody else folded. The ones who already had money in, including the blinds, all called. For a game where the average winning pot had been around $17 for the past hour or so, this surprised everyone. This pot was already at $24 and we hadn't seen a flop yet.

"Six players," I called out as I dealt and turned over the ace, the king of clubs, and the eight of spades.

Even though I was half asleep and dealing the lowest limit the Oasis offered, I was still a diehard poker player and the thought of what everyone held started to play on my imagination. To everyone's surprise, a full round of betting and raises occurred again, doubling the pot to $48, less the house rake of $3. I put one of the six on pocket aces, one of them on pocket kings, one on ace/king, one on pocket eights, and a couple of them on flush draws. How else could they stand the heat of all that betting?

The fourth card was the six of hearts, which didn't change a thing unless somebody had a pair of sixes. To keep a small pair would have been extremely foolish and unlikely. Now the betting was capped again with all six players, but this time each bet was for $3. The pot was now at $120 and even people from other tables were aware of the commotion.

The fifth card on the river was the five of diamonds.

The old man chuckled, bet $3, and said, "So much for the flush draws."

The player after him re-raised, and the old lady said, "Three bets."

Oakley lifted his cards to look at them and put them down. "That's nine dollars to me?" he asked, counting his remaining chips. He had 10 bucks left of the 30 he had started with and I couldn't help but feel sorry for the guy for going so deep on his first hand. Unless, of course, he had the pocket aces and had reeled everybody else in. As unlikely as that was, I was sort of rooting for the lieutenant. Common sense told me he was toast. I put the old pro on pocket rockets, especially after that comment about the failed flush draws.

Oakley peeked at his cards again and checked the board. He thought about it for a few seconds, counted his 10 chips out in five piles of twos, and shoved them forward. "I might as well go all in."

The small blind threw the jack and queen of clubs up in the air in frustration. "I couldn't hit a draw if my life depended on it," he yelled.

The big blind called, as did the other three.

When the smoke had settled, the old lady shouted out, "I can't take it anymore. Ace, king. Top two pair!"

The big blind smiled and threw his cards face down in front of him. "Two pairs no good. I got three eights!"

The other guy jumped out of his seat and turned over two red kings. "That don't beat a set of cowboys," he whooped.

The old pro just smiled and I knew he had what I put him on. "Send me the cookies. I flopped the nuts. Three aces."

He started accepting congratulations while he waited for his pot. I began to arrange the huge amount of chips into a pile, waiting for the lieutenant to throw in his hand.

"Excuse me," he said. "Isn't this the nuts?"

Everyone turned their heads as Oakley turned over the seven and four of hearts. Even I had to count it out in my head. "Jesus Christ . . . you've got a straight."

"Good, that's what I thought," he beamed.

The players seemed to go into a collective shock. I double-checked the board and started to push the pile his way.

"He went perfect, perfect, and got there!" someone shouted.

The old pro's eyes popped open wide and his face went red.

The guy beside him with the kings shouted, "He called four bets before the flop with a seven and four!"

The crowd oohed and awed in amazement. As I got the pile in front of Oakley, I prayed he would just take the chips and shut up. But nope, in poker there is a thing called chirping chips. Whenever a player wins a big pot, especially by luck, they tend to try to justify it to everyone. I knew this table did not want to hear a peep.

I looked over at the old man. He was visibly shaken and had broken out in sweat. He gazed at Oakley as if he were the devil.

The lieutenant began stacking his chips and I noticed his hands were shaking.

"How could you play that shit?" said the sickly looking pro.

Oakley shrugged his shoulders and proclaimed, "They were suited."

I winced and glanced at the old-timer. His mouth started making sucking motions like a fish did when you held it out of water, then his eyes stretched even wider. All of a sudden, he clutched desperately at his chest with both hands. He tried to get out of his chair, made it halfway, and collapsed forward across the green felt and his remaining chips.

"Player down!" someone called out.

The stricken man did not move. I stood and called for the floor supervisor, who was nearby. He took one look at the situation and spoke into a little microphone on his lapel and hurried over.

By the time we got the old guy on the floor ready for resuscitation, Security was on the scene. They cleared more space around him and started artificial resuscitation. I didn't like the look of things and slid the lieutenant a couple of plastic trays.

"I got a feeling this table is going to be shut down soon," I told him.

Oakley solemnly watched the guards give mouth-to-mouth, shook his head, and started to rack up his chips. Before he could finish, a couple of hotel emergency medics came running in with a respirator and took over.

McClusky showed up. "Bad beat?"

"You could say that," I told him, and pointed with a jerk of my head toward Oakley.

McClusky finally recognized the lieutenant and the two of them nodded hello.

"Well, I don't think this is going to clear up anytime soon," he said to me. "And you still look like shit. I've got some last-minute help coming in, so why don't you pack it in for the day? Try to get some rest."

"Yeah. I probably should."

Oakley finished storing his chips and the three of us watched as the medical team struggled to revive the old man. They had his shirt cut open and one of them applied a gel-like substance to the unconscious player's upper body while the other rubbed both ends of a defibrillator back and forth.

"Clear!" he called out, and pressed the paddles to the man's chest.

The body jumped, but when both medics checked their monitors, they shook their heads and tried again. After four attempts, they looked at each other grimly and began to put away their equipment. A blanket was pulled over him as the sounds of an arriving ambulance could be heard from the nearby exit.

"Tell the driver to turn off the sirens," one of the medics told a guard. "There's no hurry now. He's gone."

We all stood there in shock for at least a minute.

"Go ahead," McClusky eventually said to me. "I'll handle things here. As a matter of fact, with all the bodies that have been dropping around you lately, why don't you take a couple of days off?"

"I can't do that. I kind of need the hours."

"Don't worry. I'll put you down on the time sheet. All things considered, I don't think Mr. Contini would have a problem with that."

I wasn't a total idiot. I'd take a couple of days off with pay.

Oakley came around the table. "You off work?"

"Yeah," I answered, pulling my dealer's tray out from the table.

"Well, then let me buy you a beer?"

"It's the least you can do."

"What do you mean?"

"You never tipped me when you won, you cheapskate!"

He gave me a puzzled look. "I didn't?"

"Nope."

"Huh. Must have been all the excitement. Tell you what, I'll even spring for an imported beer."

I looked down at the blanket and the little form beneath. "Yeah, we should at least toast the poor bastard."

Oakley studied the covered shape for a second and then we started walking away. As we left, he asked me, "The hand that Wild Bill Hickok was holding when he got shot. Wasn't it aces and something?"

"The Dead Man's Hand," I said. "It was aces and eights, all black, and one hole card. Why?"

Oakley looked over his shoulder at the sight of the ambulance attendants rolling in their stretcher.

"Um," he asked pensively. "You don't think. . . ?"

Chapter

We were sitting in the Dromedary Lounge looking out over the throng of early evening gamblers.

"Well," said Oakley, as he hoisted his bottle of Moosehead and tapped it against mine. "Except for the old guy dying, that was a helluva hand, don't you think? I guess if I'm a fish, it's a great white shark."

"You were shithouse lucky, that was all. Shouldn't have even been in that hand in the first place." I took a long swallow of beer. "You're a fish all right, a great big tuna, or maybe a bottom-feeding giant catfish." I shook my head sadly. "Seven-four of hearts. Sheesh."

Oakley saluted me with his bottle and took a swig. "Don't try to rain on my parade," he said with a chuckle. "A hundred and seventy bucks in less than two minutes! I might have to start playing more often."

I smiled back. "Call me when you do. I've got lots of bills to pay."

"Or maybe I could be a barracuda," he said and looked dreamily off into the casino. "They're fierce competitors."

"Don't let it get to your head." I finished my beer and signaled the waitress for another round, on Oakley of course. "Keep playing like that and you'll be a broke little guppy."

"Yeah, right," he laughed. "And speaking of heads, what happened to yours? And the way you're walkin'. It looks like you were put through the wringer."

I took the second bottle of beer as it arrived. "Went a couple of rounds with Laura last night," I explained.

"I warned you."

Laura had made me promise to keep the events of the evening our little secret. Although I figured most of the males Laura knew had her pegged for an aggressive, racy partner, they were probably not aware of her inclination toward the dark arts.

After Oakley paid the tab, I asked him, "So what really brought you out to the Oasis?"

He folded his wad of winnings and tucked it into his pocket. "I was out here following up on the video surveillance from last Thursday night. There's been a team working on it all weekend."

"Lots of cameras," I noted. "Must have been miles of tape."

"We tried to concentrate on the hallway camera first and we had the exact time, so that wasn't so bad. Then we went to the elevator and stairway cameras. From there it was the exit units and the parking lots. The last, and most tedious, was all the floor tape. The hotel and casino floor space is about the size of three football fields and there's a camera to cover every square inch of it."

"Huge job. Did you get anything?"

"Sure. We got lots. We got the shooter coming from the east stairwell of the victim's floor and following the room service waiter, who came up the service elevator on the same side of the hotel. There's only one camera on that hallway and it's from the intersection of the four wings of the floor, so it's not a close-up. We got a guy in a light-colored, two-tone windbreaker, dark slacks and shoes, and a medium build. He's wearing a baseball cap with a logo we haven't identified yet and he wears it down low. We can't get any features.

"We backtracked his steps from camera to camera, one after another, all the way from his coming in through the main entrance about a half-hour earlier. He walked around the casino once but didn't stop to talk with anyone. He did a flyby of the poker room and used the men's room there. He came back out and got a phone call a few minutes later. From there he went up to the 20th floor, went east to the stairwell, and walked up two floors and waited for the server."

"So as soon as room service opened the door, he pushed his way in and did the waiter."

"Yup. We got him coming out, going to the elevator, and out the front entrance again. He obviously knew what he was doing. We never got a shot of his face."

"And there's been a number of these this year I heard."

"Yeah, way too many. It's a real pro with a real expensive habit or lifestyle, that's for sure."

"No prints?"

"Nothing we couldn't attribute to you, the victim, or the maids."

"Is it the same MO every time?"

"Whacking the poor room service waiter? Nah. . . . Some have been hotels, some motels, and even some homes. Most of those didn't have the security the Oasis has and we got even less. A couple of times, the robber was already in the room when the victim came in."

"And all the victims were killed?"

"All the ones who could have given a description. Some were knocked out and came to later, but those never heard or saw their attacker."

"Shy fellow," I pointed out.

"Definitely doesn't want to be recognized."

"Or maybe is too recognizable?"

Oakley thought about that for a moment. "Good point."

"And the $5,000 chip hasn't been cashed?"

"No. We've set up a plan with Security if it is. They'll be on him before the cashier is finished counting out the bills."

"Sounds like you've covered everything."

The lieutenant finished off his beer. "This guy is good. No question about it. But the hits are becoming more daring each time. One screw up, just one little lapse, and we'll have him. Trust me."

"And nothing has come up about me being there?"

"No, that's been kept hush-hush to everyone. And we haven't had any questions from anyone that could be considered prying."

"Are we going to keep it that way?"

Oakley studied me. "I think so. If we let it out it might get the killer to come out of his normal conduct, but the price for you could be rather expensive."

"Yeah, like getting myself killed."

"That's a downside, for sure." He watched for my reaction. "But you and I can talk about it later. Let's see what unfolds."

"I like that plan," I told him.

"And you haven't had any more repercussions from that scene with the Miata? No threats or anything additional in the way of action against Laura?"

"No," I said softly. "But you know there is something not kosher going on in one of Metro's departments, don't you?"

Oakley snorted and played with the remains in his bottle. "There's probably something going on, one way or another, in every police department's divisions. That's nothing new. You've always got political bullshit to deal with inside and out. You've got backstabbing peers going after your job, or the one above you. And you've got Internal Affairs sneaking up and sniffing your butt to try to nail your ass before you reach your 20th so you don't collect any benefits."

I couldn't help but laugh. "Same shit, different department."

"That'll never end."

"No," I agreed. "But you know I'm not talking about that, don't you?"
Oakley just looked at me.

"You know, Vice, in particular, has a major problem."

He pursed his lips. "I would wager that most, if not every, Vice
Department has a problem, one way or another. It comes with the terri-
tory."

"Yeah, but this one is getting real serious."

"I know. Bull and I aren't sure to what degree, but we know Laura has
to watch herself."

"I'd say machine-gun fire from a chase car is up there on the degree
chart."

Oakley's face turned serious. "Look, don't make it sound as if we aren't
doing everything we can. First off, I've got no say in what goes down in
Vice, just like Traffic has no say in what I do in Homicide. My concern is
for Laura. I already told you I've known her for a long time and I'm
impressed with her dedication to her work. Whatever is going on in Vice,
I don't think she is the cause of it. But I'm pretty sure she's caught up in
it. We have tried to talk with her, but she keeps us out of the loop. She's
told us countless times that it isn't really serious and that she can take care
of it. She doesn't want a big smear campaign that'll hurt her future, or
Metro's."

"She's a tough gal," I pointed out.

"She is that. And I don't want to see anything happen to her. I worked
with her father for a couple of years. He was a good cop who would do
anything for you. Knew her mother, too." Oakley let out a big breath. "And
I'm not so sure you hanging around with her right now is going to help
matters."

"How do you mean?"

"Look, all I can tell you is that there is a huge investigation going down now since that shootout Saturday night. It's become obvious to those upstairs that we've got some kind of rogue issue going on."

"Rogue affairs. Just a little too close to home."

"That's right. It's probably not far off from what you had going down back in Boston. Now the department is aware of it for certain. But you hanging around, as much as her uncle and I might appreciate it, it's not going to be a lot of help."

"And of course you're worried about my state of health," I said facetiously.

"Don't be a smartass, Morgan. I don't want to see you get nailed in any crossfire that could have been avoided. You have to remember, whatever it is, this isn't your fight."

"No, but they got my attention when they started shooting up the side of the car I was driving."

"Don't try to be a hero. They pulled out from a block behind you and wouldn't have even known you were in the car. They were looking for a candy-apple red Miata with Laura in it."

"Ahh," I said. "If I didn't know better, I'd think you actually care for good old Jake Morgan."

Oakley chuckled. "Don't let it go to your head, a-hole. The way bodies drop around this town when you're in the vicinity. . . . Hell, if you weren't around, my job would be a lot easier. And to tell you the truth, the way you look right now . . . I think you better start taking better care of yourself."

"Well, I don't plan on packing it in anytime soon," I told him. "But unless Laura tells me to get lost, I'm going to try to watch her back."

"You know, you must have been either a pretty good cop in a previous life, or a stubborn old mule." He glanced at his watch and stood. "I'd better head home. I'm supposed to pick up dinner for the wife and kids."

"Ah, how nice," I said as I got up from my chair. "What are you going to pick up?"

"What else?" Oakley broke out in a big, wide grin and patted his pocket of poker winnings. "Fish, of course."

Chapter

I spent the rest of Monday night and all of Tuesday morning in bed recuperating. I didn't want to see or talk to anybody; I just wanted to sleep and think about what was going down with Laura. If anyone had tried to call, I wouldn't have known. All the phone jacks were pulled. I'd had a rough week and this was my quiet time.

In the afternoon, I sat in my living room, drinking coffee and staring at the big-screen TV that wasn't turned on. A number of scenarios, some good, some not so good, came to me as to what the situation might be like within Laura's squad. Not knowing the players was a major problem in analyzing the state of affairs. After a pot of java and a couple of muffins, I finally came up with a realization; if you don't know the players, you need a program.

I did what I had to do and in an hour I was pulling into the parking lot of the Downtown Police Headquarters. A couple of cops raised an eyebrow each when they noticed the bullet holes in the side panel. Those had occurred before I officially owned the Bugatti. I decided not to have the holes filled as they made the vehicle more gangster-like. That and the fact that they were a real chick magnet.

I went into the office area and told the desk sergeant who I was there to see.

"You got an appointment with the captain?" the grizzled veteran asked, as he reached for the communication panel.

"Actually, no," I admitted.

"No appointment?" The old-timer sat back in his seat. "We'll have to make one." He looked down into a day planner. "How's Thursday around 11 a.m.?"

I smiled good-heartedly. "I'm sure The Bull will see me. It's about that shootout Saturday night after his party."

He looked up at me with renewed interest. He'd obviously heard about the incident and it brought back memories of when he was younger and had hands-on involvement in cases like that. It also looked as if it fortified my knowing Bulloch.

"You a cop?" he asked as he reached for the console again.

I gave him my "official" glare. "What do you think?"

He studied me. "Well, if you ain't, you should be."

Alexander Bulloch welcomed me into his comfortable office. He either had good taste or a good budget for office furniture as most of the pieces were antique oak and matched. The walls were decorated with a multitude of photos of The Bull with various politicians and stars. Foremost was one of him shaking hands with George Bush; in another Rodney Dangerfield presented him with a red tie. The view from the window wasn't much as it backed onto one of the hotels across the street.

"Take a seat, Jake."

There were two burgundy, leather wingback chairs in front of his wooden desk and I sat myself in the nearest one.

He leaned back into his tall recliner and smiled. "So what brings you here?" he asked. "Although I have a pretty good idea of who she probably is." He smiled even wider.

"You'd make a good cop," I told him.

He laughed at that. "Laura, Laura, Laura," he chanted. "She can be infectious to certain people."

"In a nice way, I would hope."

He nodded. "Oh, she's one of a kind, isn't she?"

I was pretty sure he was remembering her from the days when she was a little girl and used to sit on his knee and call him "Uncle Alex." He probably knew about her physical prowess in the "beating the shit out of a bunch of guys" department, but I doubted he would be too aware of her naughty, dark habits.

"She's quite the gal, for sure," I agreed. "And, yes, that's why I'm here."

"Well, what can I do for you?"

"As you might recall, I worked Vice back in Boston."

"Yes, of course. That's why I allowed you to continue to see her."

That surprised me; I didn't realize I needed his approval. I shook that one off.

"Right. Well, we all know there is something disturbing and dangerous going down in your department, specifically regarding Laura."

"Go on."

"And, as you know, after that little debacle out on the parkway Saturday night, I've decided to try to help Laura, not in an official capacity, of course, but more like a companion to watch her back, perhaps escort her here and there late at night. That sort of thing. Now don't get me wrong, I believe I could help with my experienced background — you're probably aware of a similar incident I had back —"

"I've read your file," he interrupted.

That was another traffic stopper. "You did? How the —"

"Lieutenant Oakley was kind enough to let me read it," he said. "Laura as well."

"Well, aren't I an open book," I said, in a cynical tone.

"Oh, don't be so contemptuous, Morgan. For Christ's sake, did you think for a moment that I would let you get close to her without checking you out? Wake up, man."

I shook my head. "It's just that —"

He came forward and leaned his elbows on the desk. "And, to be honest, it wasn't the most glowing of reports. If it hadn't been for the lieutenant and Laura's testimony that you've redeemed yourself from the worst of your past — except for the gambling — then I wouldn't be giving you the time of day." With that, he sat back in his chair. "Now, without all the bullshit and the beating of your chest, why is it you want to help?"

I decided to tell him what I had told Lieutenant Oakley and gave him the in-depth background story, complete with my involvement in the graft taken and up to, and including, the loss of my partner. If anything, I thought I might get a sympathetic ear to listen, and eventually a little help from Bulloch.

"That's a touching story, Morgan. If what you say is true, then Laura could be in danger if she stays in her squad, or gets promoted."

"She's in the unenviable position of damned if you do, damned if you don't."

Captain Bulloch turned his chair slightly and gave me his profile as he looked at the air-conditioning units on the roof of the building across the street. "You know, I can remember the days before the hard drugs turned the enforcement field upside down," he reflected. "Made a lot of bad cops out of good ones. From Fresno to Bangor. From the Dirty Thirty in Frisco to the Morgue Gang in the Big Apple. That shit makes it so easy for the average cop making thirty-nine nine to take home six figures, it's no wonder we've got the problems we do."

I couldn't argue the point with him.

He squinted up at the sky, pinched his nose, and swung his chair back to face me. "I've tried so damn hard to keep our division clean. My brother and I both. Gary and I were both up for captain when his plane went down, but I hadn't figured on winning that way." He smiled at some old memory. "The two of us were hellcats in Vice. They even nicknamed us Batman and Robin for all the collars we made." His face darkened. "But even then, we knew there was some bad shit going down. We did so much together because we felt so isolated from the rest of the guys. Oh, sure, they tried to sway us over earlier on, but when they saw that we weren't going to turn to extortion and robbery to fatten our wallets, we were never let into a position where we could snitch them out if we wanted to. We were left so far in the dark we could never have compiled any evidence. But we knew. And we knew the stakes were getting higher and higher."

"Did they ever give you a rough time?"

The Bull looked me in the eye. "Do you know any more than you're putting on?"

Again he caught me by surprise. "No."

He sat back and exhaled loudly. "Lieutenant Oakley knows the gist of what went on back then. He was doing a stint in Narco at the time, I think. So I don't know what he's told you and hasn't, but if you nose around here long enough or at the newspapers, you'd be able to find out anyway." The Bull held out one of his hands for inspection and flicked at a nail. "There was talk going on that it wasn't any accident the plane went down with Laura's parents. My brother was an excellent mechanic as well as pilot, and a fuel gauge that was jimmied to read full all the time wouldn't have gotten by him."

Bulloch looked like he wanted to collect his thoughts, so I let him.

"Just enough fuel," he continued, "to get up and over the Black Mountains, and then nothing. They tumbled down for almost a mile."

"That must have devastated Laura," I said. "Does she have other family?"

"No siblings, just my wife and me. We didn't have any children of our own."

"I take it there was an investigation."

"Oh, sure. The FAA were the ones that found out about the rigged gauge. The rest of the force, along with the media, went nuts with it, too. Accusations flew left and right, but nothing stuck. Internal Affairs was investigating Vice and those involved were pretty sure Gary and I had something to do with it. There were two guys in the squad that I knew must have had something to do with it. They were into the graft the worst and had the most to lose."

I held my palms out. "Sounds pretty obvious these are the guys we should be talking to about Saturday night."

Bulloch shook his head. "Not so obvious. They're both dead."

The shock must have registered on my face.

"Died a few years ago," he said. "Quite the coincidence, actually. They both were shot in the back of the head."

"Someone got the jump on both of them from behind?" I asked. "I'm astonished that two veteran cops could be nailed so easy."

"Even more amazing, they were both sitting in the front seat of their unmarked car. The shooter plugged both of them from the back seat with a different caliber each. For sure somebody they trusted."

"Or never would have suspected," I added.

"That, too."

If I hadn't been sitting in the same room talking with him, my money would have been on The Bull for pulling the triggers. But the last thing he looked was proud.

"So they never found the gunman?" I asked.

"Nope." He was watching me watching him. "And if by that look you're giving me, Morgan, you think it was maybe me . . . you're wrong. Hell," he snorted, "if it was me, I'd be giving you a big old wink. Believe me."

I did.

"The only blight on my career is not cleaning up the department entirely. Oh, don't get me wrong, I got a number of bad apples discharged, but the infection ran very deep. And it's not hard to imagine. Look at this city: the fastest growing per capita in North America for more than 10 years now. And think of all the losers that are drawn here for the fast money and fast women — present company excluded, of course. It's been a powder keg waiting to explode since the days Hughes ran The Strip." He shook his head sadly. "But Laura was like a daughter to my wife, God rest her soul, and I wouldn't be able to handle it if anything happened to her."

"And that's why I want to help," I told him. "I might be able to get into places you guys can't. People in your unit don't know my face, but I might recognize a few of their voices and be able to put names to them. You'd be a big help if you could get me a roster of your squad going back five years or so. And photos if you have them."

The Bull looked at me and shook his head. "I must be nuts to be getting involved with an outsider like you. And right before my retirement." He pointed a finger at me. "Look, I'm still judging you on what I've heard from Lieutenant Oakley and Laura. If I decide to let you help, it'll be on my terms: you keep the lieutenant and me informed on anything you come up with, no matter how insignificant. You watch Laura's back and protect her at all costs or don't bother to get involved. But remember, no guns. That's a no-can-do. I won't be able to help you out of any weapons charges. And lastly, you remember that this is a fishing expedition, just try to gather some information. Don't go running off half-cocked trying to be some kind of cowboy."

"You can rest easy," I assured him. "I've never even been on a horse."

Bulloch studied me some more. "Off the record, I appreciate what you're doing for Laura."

"For the record," I told him softly, "I'm doing it for myself, too. I've got some old debts in the conscience department that need paying off. Then maybe I'll be able to sleep better at night."

The elderly cop nodded. "I hear you."

"And you'll be able to give me what I need?"

"I've got your address in your file," he said. "There'll be a package on your doorstep before dark. As far as I'm concerned, the photos will be the most important. At least you'll have something to go by visually if you run into any of them. Nothing original, only copies, and I won't admit knowing anything about it if I'm asked."

"Gotcha."

The two of us sat silent for a moment, then he said, "There's nothing I'd like more than to see closure on these threats to Laura and the murder of her parents."

"That's understandable," I told him.

He looked me steadfastly in the eyes. "There's a little more to the story of the plane going down that not many people know about."

"What's that?"

Alexander Bulloch looked at me grimly. "We had planned this trip for quite a while, and a lot of people knew it. My wife and I were supposed to be on that plane, too."

Chapter

I'd laid a few baseball bets down at the Barbary Coast and was sitting at home playing online poker when the telephone rang.

"Hello?" I answered, ready to blow off some telemarketer.

A male voice responded, "Door," and then the connection was cut.

I went to the front door of my two-story condo and opened it wide. There on the step was a 10x13 manila envelope. I picked up the package and looked down at the yard and along the street without seeing anyone who could have been the delivery person.

I closed the door, locked it, and went into the kitchen, where I poured the contents of the envelope onto the table. There were six sheets of names, addresses, and telephone numbers, one for each year's Vice roster starting with the year 2000. Two dozen or so photos of standard ID size were bound together by elastics.

I started with the oldest list and worked my way to the current one. There were anywhere from 15 to 20 names on each, and I noticed that for the most part, the names didn't change. There was the odd transfer to Narcotics or Robbery, but I wasn't interested in those. I found what I was looking for when I located three names that had DECEASED printed beside them. Two were marked as having died from gunshot wounds back in November of 2001 and their names were Anthony Rinaldo and Jerry Ball. The third was Vladimir Kasparitis.

I shuffled through the photos like I was sorting through a deck of cards, trying to find anyone I might recognize. A couple looked familiar, as if I might have seen them at the retirement party, but one, in particular, stood out from the rest. It was the large black cop who had joked around with me when I was dealing on Saturday. The one with no neck. The one I could have sworn resembled the silhouette I saw when I was hiding out in the men's room. I read his name and filed it in my brain: Parker. Theodore Parker. And probably the Teddy Bear that had been referred to by one of the conspirators.

I remembered this being how most investigations got off the ground: a name here, a reference there. Like a puzzle, it had to start somewhere, and it always started with the first piece fitting in with the second. I was on my way.

I also knew from my own experience that most cops were like poker players; many of them had nicknames to set the individuals apart. Some of the guys I played cards with had monikers as simple as Kid Poker, Big Bob, Little Bob, Fast Eddie, Chinese Dave, and JB, JR, or JT. Then you had those that were a little more abstract. Like Wallbanger, for the guy named Harvey, AK47 for the guy who always raised with Big Slick, or Stinky, which pretty much explained itself.

And then you had the big 300 pound cops named Theodore who were affectionately known as Teddy Bear.

I started going up and down the lists, stopping here and there when I thought I might have something. After a row of double-filled Oreos and two glasses of milk, I came up with a couple more I thought were a match.

The first was Carl Ratinski, who I was pegging as "The Rat" also referred to in the locker room last Saturday night. The second came to me pretty easy. The unseen plotters that evening had also mentioned someone named "Spooky," whom they had probably taken out. I stopped at Kasparitis, not only because the deceased's name, Kaspar, could translate to Casper and then shift to the ghostly nickname of Spooky — but it was also the name of the forlorn-looking woman I had met when I had donated my tips at The Bull's retirement party.

By this time, my brain was getting a little foggy and I was having trouble keeping my eyes open. I knew I had come up with references on at least three members of the squad and it would be enough of a starting point. I also knew I had a few aches and pains to take care of with a good night's rest. I closed the file, turned out the lights, and headed off to bed.

Chapter

By 11 a.m. Wednesday morning, I had the Bugatti's nose pointed west on Spring Mountain Road and my own beak aimed down at a MapQuest printout I'd made looking for Meadow Brook Lane.

I finally found my turn-off and a few minutes later I pulled into a driveway with the big black numbers 1243 posted over a single, white garage door. The area was new, upper middle class, out of reach for a single dealer, but fit for an up-and-coming casino exec. Or a cop on the pad.

I circumvented a couple of tricycles, a wagon, and a jumbo yellow plastic baseball bat on the sidewalk to the front steps. As I approached the door, a yappy little white-haired terrier barked to announce my arrival. A couple of young kids, a boy and a girl, followed, and they, too, made it known that I was there. I smiled at the welcoming committee and made funny until their mother and master arrived to shush everybody. The hairy one obeyed instructions but kept his bottom row of front teeth bared to make sure I toed the line.

"Hello, Mrs. Kasparitis," I said. "I'm Jake Morgan. I called earlier."

"Yes, I remember your face from the retirement party. Please, call me Helena. Come in."

I entered the crowded foyer and was immediately hit by a terrific aroma.

"Something smells good," I commented.

Helena wiped her hands on her flowered apron. "Fresh bread, and borscht."

"Borscht?" I asked with a raised brow.

"Yes, it is a Russian soup."

The children were not interested in our chit-chat and began tugging at each other.

"Okay, I want you both to be good while I talk with Mr. Morgan," she instructed them. "Sasha, take your sister and go to the TV room. I set up *Finding Nemo*. All you have to do is start it."

"Nemo, Nemo, Nemo!" the young girl shouted as she ran down the hall, followed by her brother. The fur ball took one look at Helena to make sure she wasn't in danger, and then scampered down the hall in pursuit of the children, or perhaps Nemo.

The heady smell was overwhelming when we entered the kitchen.

"Take a seat."

I sat down at a thick, round, oak table for four that overlooked a medium-sized backyard filled with toys and a giant slide and swing set. Helena poured coffee into two large ceramic mugs and offered me milk and sugar, which I declined. She took a moment to check the oven window and to stir the contents of a tall aluminum pot, then she took a seat across from me.

She was an attractive woman in her mid-30s, average height, average weight, with long dark hair that fell below her shoulders. She'd be a whole lot more attractive, I thought, if she could exchange her perpetual sadness for just the trace of a smile. But then again, I wasn't walking in her shoes carrying around two young kids with no father.

"So, did you work with Vlad?" she asked. "You didn't tell me how you knew my husband."

"No, I didn't work with him."

She sipped at her hot coffee. "But you are police?"

"I used to be. Not anymore."

She nodded over her cup. "It's in your eyes, you know. I've seen it in the men Vlad worked with. Not totally soulless, but they look like they've seen more distress than the average man, twice their age."

"Seen their share," I agreed. I took a sip and held out my mug. "Wonderful."

"Thank you. Freshly ground beans. Dark Colombian."

I acknowledged that with a nod, then after a moment said, "But, yes, Helena, I did the work your husband did, but a long time ago in a far different place."

A timer went off on the stove and Helena excused herself. She pulled a pan of buns from the oven and placed them on the counter where I could get a whiff of them.

"And why are you here?" she asked, resuming her seat.

"Well, I have a friend who worked with Vladimir, not closely, but in the same department. This person has run into trouble at work and I am afraid there may be danger."

"I see," said Helena as she took another drink. "And you think your friend might be killed by the same police that killed Vlad?"

The shock surely registered on my face, but I couldn't help it and didn't care. "Excuse me?"

Her eyes appeared moist. "There!" she hissed vehemently. "I have said it. I am no longer afraid."

"Please, Helena. What you just said about the police. . . ."

She crossed her arms and struck a defiant pose. "I said what I feel and what I know. The men Vlad worked with . . . they made me a widow."

"Take your time," I told her. "Tell me why you say that."

She wiped a tear from her eye and collected herself. "I say it because it is what I know happened to my husband. He warned me many times that there was trouble happening in his work. Not just the trouble he had as a policeman with his job, but with the other men."

"Start at the beginning, Helena. How long was Vladimir on Vice?"

She wrapped both hands around her mug as if to stay warm. "He was with Las Vegas police for almost seven years. He came from Russia for a one-year trial, to work on a project here that involved men from what they call the Russian Mafia. We were not married when he left, but later he sent me airplane ticket and Metro made it easy for us to get all the proper papers so we could stay here. We were married like the tourists here: at a chapel on The Strip one year after.

"Those early years, they were so wonderful. Coming from Russia to a city like Las Vegas . . . there is nothing in the world that could be much more opposite. Vlad was making more money than we could ever dream of and life was so good — stores filled with food, no bitter winters. We decided to have our children and stay here forever."

She sipped slowly from her mug. "And then about two years ago, things with my husband changed. He was not the same man when he came home from work. Where he once would spend time with me and the children playing games, reading, watching television, now he would go off on his own. I would find him sitting with a bottle of vodka in the backyard staring at the fence. Or down in the basement.

"I tried so many times to talk with him but never got an explanation. Then I noticed money being put into our bank account that I did not know about: two thousand, fifteen hundred, three thousand — always rounded-off amounts. When I asked my husband about this, he was shocked, and then he was angry. I thought the extra money was wonderful, but Vlad explained that it wasn't ours and not to spend any of it. I begged him to explain what was going on, and in the end he told me that there was dishonesty in his work and with the people he worked with. He explained how there was always the temptation to take some of the money, jewelry, or drugs that were seized on jobs and no one would ever know. He told me he told them that *he* would know and that he did not want anything to do with what they were doing. We both loved this country and were proud to be citizens, but we were not here to rob and steal like those who were oppressing us back in mother Russia. Vlad promised me he didn't put that money in but that somebody had to make it look that way. He told me he would take care of it and everything would be fine."

Another timer went off and Helena got up, walked to the stove, and turned off the burner that the soup was on. She retrieved two children's bowls and ladled them with the borscht, then she took two buns from the pan on the countertop and put everything on a tray. "Excuse me for a moment."

I sat, deeply inhaling the rich aromas turning on my olfactory nerves. Fortunately I was saved the embarrassment of asking for a serving when Helena re-entered the kitchen and asked if I would like some lunch.

"If it's no bother," I told her.

She smiled ever so slightly and it affected her entire appearance. "Your hungry face made me think of how much Vlad liked my cooking." She took a larger bowl down from a cupboard and proceeded to fill it. "It's nice to have a man here to cook for."

Helena brought the bowl over to the table and placed it in front of me, along with a large spoon and a cloth napkin.

"So this is borscht," I said. "I don't think I've ever eaten purple soup before."

"It's made from beets, a staple in the Russian diet," she said, as she returned from the counter with a basket of fresh buns.

I took one, held it close to my nose, and inhaled as I broke it open. "Mmm."

Helena went to the refrigerator and came back with a white container. "Try some of the borscht, then put in a few spoonfuls of sour cream. You'll taste quite a difference."

I did as I was told and found the experiment to be a success. "Exquisite. And so are the rolls. My compliments to the chef."

"It is my grandmother's recipe, passed down from her mother. I will make sure she gets your best wishes when I talk with her next."

She took her seat and I could tell she was enjoying me enjoying myself, then she continued where she had left off.

"My Vlad told me it would be fine, but it wasn't. One night he came home very late and I found him sitting in the dark, here in the kitchen. He was not one to let me worry, but I knew things must be very bad because he told me to sit and listen to what he had to say."

I put my spoon down and used the last of my bread to sop up the remaining soup.

"Let me get you some more."

"No, thank you. It was delicious but, please, carry on."

"My husband told me he had problems with some of the men he worked with. There was a group that was working outside the law." Her brow furrowed. "There was a name he called it, but it was strange and I didn't know what it meant."

"Rogue?"

Her eyes went wide. "Yes, that is it. They were a rogue unit, to make more money for each of them. He said this group wanted him to join, but he told them he wouldn't. As I told you, we were feeling very lucky to be here, and did not want to do something illegal, and lose everything we had worked for."

"Strange that they would be that desperate that they would go to such lengths to have him join. It's my experience that if someone didn't want to join such a unit, they would just be forgotten, not threatened."

"I was thinking the very same," said Helena. "But Vlad told me that this was a job that was special to him only."

She saw the confusion on my face.

"Yes, Vlad said that this unit had some big business with a group of Russians who were slowly getting into some very rich situations for all of them. They wanted Vlad to act as an undercover translator in case the truth was not being spoken when the Russians spoke their native tongue to each other. And they also thought his background in the Russian police would be an advantage in dealing with these gangsters, who were promising a lot of money to be spread around."

"That would be smart," I said. "It makes sense now."

"Vlad was worried that they would not take no for answer. He said the trail of money they were laying on him was to scare him of being falsely accused. They told him they would go to their supervisors and tell them that he was one of the ones stealing from crime scenes and being paid off by criminals."

Helena's tone dropped as she continued. "All this trouble didn't matter in the end though. The next night, my husband did not come home when he said he would. Instead, a captain and a police lady were at the door when I answered."

"I'm so sorry. . . ."

She looked off into the backyard and a solitary tear rolled slowly down her cheek.

"They said his unit had gone into a crack house to capture a wanted criminal that was believed to be there. They said he shot my Vladimir and that they then killed him."

They *said* being the key word. There weren't many vice cops that I knew that didn't carry a throwaway piece for special occasions. Some carried two. The bad guy in question could have easily been so stoned he was walking with Alice in a place called Wonderland and didn't even feel it when they unloaded bullets into him. Vlad could have been shot by his buddies with a throwaway before, or after, and then have that same gun put into the druggy's hand for print detection. It happened all the time, but I wasn't going to tell Helena that.

And almost as if she had read my mind, she said, "I know what you are thinking."

I didn't say a word.

"You know there are many ways to falsify a shooting like the one my husband died in. It could have been a set-up and they sent Vlad in that doorway first, knowing there was someone waiting there with a gun. To cover it up, the police would have shot the shooter. Case conveniently closed."

I still had nothing to say that could help.

"Or, if my husband was truly in trouble with his group . . . well, I know they could have made it to look the way they reported.

"My husband died in the line of duty and was given full honors for his burial. Police from all over came to attend. It has been just over a year now and the children were so young they didn't understand all the festivity. I was in shock and barely made it through the first month. If it hadn't been for the children, I'm not sure what I would have done. . . ."

"I really am so sorry," I said, and took her hand in mine. "I lost someone very close to me in a very similar way. I know how you must have felt."

She looked at me and studied my eyes. "Yes," she said. "I can feel it when I look at you."

"I assume the force took care of everything?"

"Oh, yes, they were very good that way. The house is paid off and I get all of Vlad's benefits. His insurance made sure that the children's education will not suffer."

"And what about you?"

"Me? I still haven't gone through all the stages the counselors said I'd need to go through, but I am holding on. The children are the glue keeping me together. For now, everything I do is for them. Perhaps when they are both in school full-time in another year, I'll find myself a part-time job to keep busy. Make some extra money. We'll see."

"And you're doing a wonderful job here already, Helena. You will be fine. I know you will."

I got up from the table. "Thank you for sharing the events that went on in your husband's squad. The information you gave me could end up being very helpful to the safety of my friend. And thank you for a delicious lunch. It was wonderful."

"You are more than welcome, and I will be most proud if I could be of any help to your friend. This is such a difficult city just to live in, so many temptations. To have to work in the same environment makes it that much worse. Give my best to your friend. If you can, let me know how it works out."

For a second, I didn't know if that was an invitation to see her again or not.

"Thanks again."

As I turned to leave, she placed a hand on my arm. "Jake?"

"Yes?"

"Is there something you want to ask me?"

Now I was really confused. And a little afraid she may have misread my intentions. "I, uh . . . is there?"

The corners of her mouth lifted fractionally. "Would it be easier if I asked it?"

My mouth went dry. I really wasn't ready for another relationship. "Um, sure, I guess."

"Okay, here goes," she announced. "Jake?"

"Yes?"

"Would you like to take a bowl of soup and a bun home with you?"

"Oh, Helena," I exclaimed and gave her a short hug. "Bless your heart."

Chapter

There was a message from Laura on my machine when I got back.

"Hi there, big boy, it's your Mistress calling. I'm going to work tonight around eight, so meet me for dinner at seven. At the Denny's at Fremont and East Charleston."

Denny's?

"That's right, Denny's," she continued, as if predicting my surprise. "And it's not just because it's in your price range to pay for dinner this time. I'll explain later."

I went back to online poker for the next few hours and managed to lower my $1,800 bankroll down to under a $1,000. The action had been fast and furious but mostly frustrating as most of my money had gone to two players who claimed to have learned the game the day before. So much for my poker pride.

◆

The restaurant, known more for its cheap breakfasts, wasn't very busy when I arrived. A group of male Japanese tourists involved in a loud discussion took up a table for eight, a few locals looking down on their luck were scattered about, and a hooker with long red curly tresses sat in a booth by herself. The package was put together and displayed to get maximum attention. She was wearing skimpy, pink hot pants, black stiletto heels, and a tight, almost sheer, halter top that made it blatantly obvious she was wearing nothing underneath.

I checked my watch, which showed I was on time and sat on a red leather stool at the counter. A tired waitress came by and poured coffee into the upturned cup in front of me without asking. She slid a laminated menu my way and told me she'd be back in two shakes of a lamb's tail, whatever the hell that meant.

The coffee was better than I expected and I picked up a tattered sports section of *U.S.A. Today* to check on the baseball bets I'd laid down at the Barbary the day before.

I heard the click of heels coming my way from the booth area and a sultry voice say, "Hey, good lookin'. Gotta light?"

Great, I thought. *This is all I need.* "Don't smoke," I said disinterestedly.

Her perfume was overpowering and intensely stimulating as I felt her lean over and press a breast into my shoulder.

"Are you a rocket scientist?" she asked, from somewhere out in left field.

"Ah, not exactly," I answered, burying my nose deeper in the paper.

She ran a fingernail up my thigh in a zigzag pattern. "Well, I bet I could launch your missile, big boy."

The *big boy* reference sounded vaguely familiar, but I was afraid to lift my head to make eye contact with her. I decided to get up and change seats. As I did so she grabbed my ass in her hand.

"Or we could take a trip to Uranus," she suggested.

Enough was enough. I turned and grasped her wrist, ready to escort her ass out the door. "Look, this is a family rest—"

That was all I got out. The next thing I knew my arm was turned around and my hand was somewhere up the middle of my back. Admittedly, it had been a number of years since my last hand-to-hand combat lesson, but still, I shouldn't have been bested by some woman. And a common hooker at that.

"Jesus!" I yelled out. "That hurts."

I could see that none of the locals paid us any attention, but the Asian contingent were mildly amused and started pulling out their cameras. As if posing for the paparazzi, my potential lover/attacker planted her moist lips on my neck and started to nibble with her teeth. A chorus of camera flashes went off.

She bit me lightly and cooed, "Sometimes hurtin' love is the best love."

I pulled my head away and looked at her. "Laura?"

She smiled brightly. "That's Mistress Laura to you."

I shook myself free. "What's with the getup?" I asked in amazement. "And the red hair?"

"I told you I had to work tonight," she explained as she placed her hands on her hips and jutted out her chest. "You like?"

I looked around the restaurant. "Jesus, Laura. This is embarrassing."

She thought that was funny, reached over and picked up my coffee, and went back to the booth shamelessly emphasizing the wiggle in her walk.

I shook my head and followed as the room erupted in another round of flashes.

We sat across from each other, me chastising her with my cop look while she made a steeple out of her fingers, rested her chin on her hands, and batted her big fake eyelashes at me.

"You could have just called me over when I came in, you know," I told her.

"Oh, come on, Jake. What kind of fun would that have been?"

"My kind."

We stared each other down and I finally gave in and started smiling.

"You got me good," I admitted.

"What can I say?" she said. "I'm good at what I do."

The waitress came over with her pad and pen. "Hey, Laura. How's tricks?"

The two of them started to laugh like a couple of schoolgirls.

"That's a trade joke," Laura explained to me.

We all had a good chuckle over that and then the waitress asked, "So, this your new partner, Laura?"

"No, he used to be a cop," she said. "Not anymore."

"I been serving bad coffee and questionable food to Metro cops for 23 years," she said, squinting at my face. "You sure coulda fooled me."

"Jake's his name, Connie."

"Well, I knew he wasn't a *John*," she stated, and they had another hoot over that.

"I'll have the chicken cacciatore and a basket of garlic cheese bread, Connie."

She scribbled my order down and then asked Laura, "The usual, hon?"

"Jake's buying," Laura said. "So I think I'll splurge. Make it three eggs scrambled instead of two."

"Nice," Connie said. "I can see you've got yourself a real big spender." She wrote that order down on her pad as well and walked over to the group of tourists.

"Scrambled eggs?" I asked. "For dinner?"

"Are you kidding, Jake?" Laura said. "Did you get a look at those guys working the grill back there?"

"What do you mean?" I asked, my salmonella radar rising.

"It's like some kind of inbreeding experiment by the descendants of the Marx Brothers," she explained. "I made the mistake once of ordering alphabet soup and I got a warm bowl of Cheerios."

I noticed the waitress returning to the kitchen. "Connie," I called out. "Make mine the same as hers."

She crossed out my order on her pad and replied, "Good choice."

"So," I said to Laura. "I take it you're working undercover tonight."

"No," she said facetiously. "I always dress up like this when I walk the streets."

"Are things that slow that your squad does solicitation duty in the middle of the week?"

"Nah, there's more to it than that," she said, now very serious. "Three pavement pros have been sexually mutilated in the last two months near here. We're trying to fish the perv out."

I looked down at her gaping cleavage and said, "Judging from what I see, you're using the right bait. But that kind of assignment can be dangerous."

"Well, this guy is a serious psycho. You don't want to know what he's doing to these girls after they're cold."

I sipped at my coffee. "I can imagine."

"It's the worst. We need to get this guy off the streets while it's still only local news. We've got enough problems downtown without the Chamber of Commerce worrying about a national story breaking about how Vegas has a serial killer on the loose."

We made some small talk about the rigors and dangers of a takedown like this and exchanged stories of encounters from our pasts. Laura told me she was working with one of the few guys in her squad she totally trusted and didn't seem overly worried about her assignment. She also told me a bunch of the boys were getting together later that night at a stag for a guy in Gang Enforcement at a downtown bar called O'Reilly's.

Our food came and we dug in, while Laura reiterated the highlights of our little romp into her world of bondage and pain. I just ate and listened and noted how worked up she became the more she talked about it.

"Jesus, I'm horny," she said as she finished her eggs and wiped her mouth with a napkin.

"Maybe it's the getup," I reasoned and smiled.

"You know, you might be right," she said. "I do like playing the part."

"Ah, a star is born."

"Yeah, a porno star." Laura had a peculiar look about her as she turned her head and surveyed the room. "You wanna give those tourists a Kodak moment?"

I looked at the octet as they ate their meal and kept an eye on our booth as if another ruckus might break out.

"You're not thinking what I think you're thinking, are you?" I asked nervously.

She smiled back at me and bit lightly on her bottom lip. "Let's do it, Jake."

"You mean the proverbial *it?*" I asked with a raised brow.

"Yes," she said hotly. "Right here."

I looked at her as if she'd lost her mind. "Laura, it's a Denny's for Christ's sake!"

"That's what makes it hotter," she explained. A spasm seemed to course through her and she trembled. "God, I think I just came thinking about it."

"Jesus, Laura, get a hold of yourself," I told her.

"That won't do," she protested. "Besides, I did that an hour ago while I was getting dressed and saw how hot I looked in the mirror. No, I need the real thing."

"You can't be serious," I told her. "If I'd had it an hour ago, I'd still be asleep."

"Don't you know that's the difference between men and women?"

"I know I'm supposed to be from Mars and you're supposed to be from Venus," I said, although I wanted to add that she was definitely from another planet.

"I'm serious, Jake," she confirmed as she closed her eyes and shuddered again. "Oh, my God, it's a multi!"

"You okay?" I asked.

"I will be as soon as you put out the fire." She opened her eyes and wet her lips. "Come on, don't be a prude. Let's hit the lady's room. If you want we can make a game out of it."

"A game?"

"Yes. You go outside, come back in, and sit down at the counter again. We'll pretend we don't know each other and I'll come over and hustle you. Those guys with the cameras will go nuts."

"Forget it," I said. "I'm not making love in some restaurant washroom."

"Who said anything about love? Don't be such a romantic. I just want sex. Fast and dirty."

"Well, I can usually guarantee fast," I said. "And it is a restaurant, so it's just about a given it'll be dirty. . . ."

"Very funny," Laura said with a pout. "Don't you care about me?"

"Sure I do," I insisted. "And while I admit your lovemaking, um, I mean sex, is infectious, I don't want either one of us to catch anything transmittable."

Laura thought about that for a minute and it seemed to do the job. She let out a big sigh. "Maybe you're right," she said and looked again at the tourists and then back at me as if she had just come up with a great idea. "Jake, open the newspaper and hang it from the end of the table."

Anything to get her mind off the restroom antics she had suggested. I took the sports section, opened it, and draped it off the end of the booth.

"Like this?" I asked, feeling foolish.

"Perfect," she said.

"Now what?"

"Now just sit there and drink your coffee while I slip under the table."

I grabbed the newspaper back and proceeded to fold it. "Will you give it up?"

"Sheesh," she said, as she grabbed a cigarette from her purse and lit it. "I've never met a guy so hung up. . . ."

"Hung up?" I said. "I'm not hung up. I'm . . . I'm just . . . controlled. Doing it at a Denny's is just . . . it's just wrong."

"Oh, don't get your tits in a wringer, sweetie," she said with a smile. "I was just fuckin' with you."

I studied her sincerity. "You mean you weren't really going to go under the table? Or do it in the restroom?"

Laura screwed up her face. "Are you kidding? That washroom is gross. And I'm not going to tear the knees in my nylons on the crappy floor here in the booth."

"Why you little teaser," I chastised. "So even those little shudders and that trembling —"

"Oh, no," she exclaimed. "That part was real. I actually got off remembering the other night." She dragged on her cigarette and blew a cloud my way. "The rest of it . . . I was just jerking your chain."

Connie came over and asked if we'd like anything else. We said no and as she left the check on the table, a car pulled up out front and screeched its tires as it whipped to a stop.

The tired waitress looked over her shoulder at the noise and shook her head sadly.

"Here's Starsky," she said and walked away.

"That's Billy," corrected Laura. "My partner tonight."

We both watched as Billy got out of the dark-colored, unmarked squad car, came over to the sidewalk, and did a James Dean pose against the fender. He looked to be in his 20s and had a good head of black hair slicked back with lots of gel. If he was a true traditionalist, I guessed it would be Brylcreem if they still made the stuff. He put on a pair of aviator glasses, took a pack of smokes from under his rolled-up T-shirt sleeve, and fired it up with a flick of what had to be a big, old, silver Zippo lighter.

I glanced over at Laura with a great amount of skepticism.

"He's kinda new."

"And young," I added.

"That, too," she concurred as she got up from the booth and slid the check my way. "Your turn."

I paid the modest bill and left Connie a fat tip.

As we approached the group of Asian tourists, they all stopped eating and watched as Laura sashayed her way toward the exit. They started yammering in their own language and poking each other with their elbows. One of them was making like a walleye as he pursed his lips and blew air as he tried to make a wolf-whistle. His buddy, encouraged by his friend's antics, licked his own lips like it was supposed to be sexy, squeezed his skinny chest, and called out, "Hey, baby!"

A stout fellow closest to the aisle must have been the spokesman for the group as he called out something in Japanese as Laura neared. To emphasize whatever it was he was saying, he made a circle using the first finger and thumb of his left hand and proceeded to insert the index finger of his right hand in and out of the other. The rest of the gang found this outrageously funny.

When Laura stopped at his side to see what was so humorous, he said something else to her and followed it up with a suggestive wink. He took out his billfold, removed a one dollar bill, and offered it to her. Somebody took a picture and two more flashes lit up Laura's annoyed facial features. If it had been a cartoon, a steam whistle would have sounded, and smoke would have come from her ears.

Oh, oh, I thought. I felt around in my pocket for my cellphone with the camera feature as it looked like a photo op was about to transpire.

Fortunately Billy was checking himself out in the side-view mirror and hadn't seen the exchange. He might have started firing through the plate-glass window.

Laura leaned over and grabbed the comedian's wrist. The rest of them shut the hell up. She pointed his shaking index finger in the air and started to lay into him so verbally that her spittle sparkled on his black-framed glasses. The interesting part of all this was that she spoke in Japanese. They were so shocked, or scared, that no one dared take a picture.

When she had made whatever point it was she was making, she let go of the guy's hand, saw me with the camera phone, and placed her face beside his.

"Jake, take a full shot of us on the count of three," she said.

I aimed the lens at the two of them and waited.

"One, two. . . ."

Prior to the count of three Laura planted a big wet kiss on him, leaving a bright red lip outline on his cheek. She put her smiling face against his startled one and grabbed his crotch with her hand.

"Three," she sang out.

I took the shot.

Laura let go of his package, picked up his wallet, and removed a business card, then she ripped into him verbally once more, and stormed off.

When I caught up with her at the door, I asked, "What the hell did you say to him?"

The corner of her mouth turned up to form the tiniest of smiles. "I told him all eight of their little pencil dicks couldn't satisfy a hot American woman like me."

"You didn't!" I said, even though I knew she probably had.

Her smile enlarged fractionally. "And when you took our picture? I told him I was a cop and was going to track his wife down and send her the picture of us two."

"You're an evil woman, Laura Bulloch."

She studied me for a moment. "Not to mention dangerous," she added.

I shook my head in amazement. "Where the hell did you learn to speak Japanese?"

"My uncle took me to a police conference in Tokyo a year ago. I fell in love with the city and took some time to study their culture and language. I don't speak it fluently, but I can get by in a basic conversation."

"That, my dear," I told her, "was anything but basic."

At the door, we glanced back. The locals had returned to their meals, while a couple of the Asian contingent consoled their humiliated comrade.

"Come on," Laura said.

I held the door for her and we went out to the sidewalk, where we beheld a very strange sight.

Billy had his piece out and was holding it in both hands in the classic isosceles shooting stance: arms partially bent and extended symmetrically, feet squared slightly wider than shoulder width, support foot slightly forward, and the balance on the balls of the feet. The only thing wrong with this picture was that he was aiming at the center of my chest. That and the fact that his hands shook so much I had to pray his gun didn't have a hair trigger.

"Hold it right there, motherfucker!"

I froze where I was and held my arms out so he could see my hands were empty.

"Everything's cool, Fonzie," I said in a reassuring tone. "Don't jump the shark."

Chapter

"Billy!" Laura screamed. "What the hell do you think you're doing?"

The nervous young cop kept his Glock aimed at me as his eyes skittered back and forth from me to Laura.

"I thought you met up with the guy we're looking for," yelled back Billy.

"Easy there, buddy boy," I said. "You got the wrong perv."

"Jesus Christ, Billy," Laura chastised. "Put the damn gun away. This is a friend of mine."

Billy's body relaxed and his hands stopped shaking. "You mean. . . ."

"That's right," she said, as she stepped between the gun and the target.

"But I thought. . . ."

"Did you see me give you the signal?"

"Well, no. . . ."

Laura shook her head. "Get in the car, Billy."

The kid put his piece back under the back of his T-shirt and sheepishly glanced over at me. "Sorry, dude." He walked around the back of the car and got inside.

Laura came over. "You all right?" she asked.

I waved it off. "No problem. I'm fine."

"That's good," she said, cocking her head on an angle with an inquisitive look on her face. "Then how come you wet yourself?"

"I what?" I shouted, looking down at the front of my pants and finding them perfectly dry.

"Ah, I was just fucking with you," she explained with a laugh. "Hey, that
reminds me, you owe me a raincheck for not letting me ride the pony in
there."

"But you have to work."

"I know, and that's just it. Can you imagine how horny I'm going to be
after a couple of hours of shaking my ass for every guy that'll look at it?"

Billy started up the car.

"I'll be going out for a while tonight," I told her. "Maybe for a drink."

"Good, you do that. Hit a peeler bar too, while you're at it. Stoke the
fire for me."

"Sure," I laughed back. "I'll see what I can do."

Laura opened the car door and got in. Her shorts, or what there were
to them, rode halfway up her ass. "Hey, no window shopping," she yelled
at me with a grin. "I'll call you on your cell and you can come over to my
place."

"You mean your house?" I asked. "You've decided to move back in?"

Laura shut the door and rolled down the window. "Yeah, I decided not
to run scared anymore. Besides, you'll be there to protect me. And that's
where I keep all my heavy-duty toys."

"Oh, great," I feigned. "Lucky me."

"You don't know how lucky you are," she shouted as the car began to
roll away. "I could have given Billy the signal when we came out."

Since I was already downtown, I decided to go over to the Golden Nugget
and play some cards. With the closure of Binion's Horseshoe and the current poker craze in full swing, the Nugget had reopened its card room to

great fanfare. I spent the next few hours dodging gut-shot straights and perfect-perfect flush draws, and managed to eke out a modest win. When I'd had enough of the young guns and their elastic-bound bankrolls, I hiked the two blocks to my next destination.

O'Reilly's did its best to look like an Irish pub in the middle of the Mojave Desert. There was a big oak bar down one side as you walked in and a row of booths down the other. At the end was a section of tables with a small stage. Just past that was an area holding three pool tables and a private party room. A few locals sat at the bar nursing their drinks while a red-headed, burly bartender wiped at a spot on the bar.

Since I was here presumably as a cop, I thought I might as well show off my police proclivities. I noticed his green shirt had the name "Paddy" stitched in above the pocket.

"You O'Reilly?" I asked in an official tone.

The bartender looked up at me. "No, I'm Stanislovkowski," he said in a heavy brogue accent.

I looked at the name on the shirt again. "Come on, you gotta be shittin' me. Paddy Stanislovkowski?"

He flipped his little white towel over and started wiping once more. "Used to be O'Stanislovkowski. I dropped the 'O' to shorten it."

One of the locals at the bar snorted into his beer like he'd heard this before but still found it funny. I wanted to keep up my cop image so I didn't join in the frivolity.

"You here for the Leon Tang stag?" Paddy asked.

"No," I answered, leaning against the bar. "I'm here to trace your family tree."

Now the local laughed so hard he broke wind with great fanfare.

Paddy waved his white towel as if to clear the air. "Yeah, you're a cop all right. You all think you're comedians." He placed the towel over his wide left shoulder. "Your buddies are in the back. But there's no bar there. You have to order here. What'll it be? A watered-down, horse-piss, American beer?"

I was glad my cover was holding up, but I was ticked off at the derogatory homeland comment. I might be half Irish, but I was 100 percent American. "Gimme a pint of Guinness. I'm feeling rather gay and reckless. Or would that be . . . *Gae*-lic?"

Paddy looked up at me sternly. "You can't order that, my good man."

"Oh? And why not?"

His face assembled in great shock. "Why, that's a man's beer!" This was followed by a hearty laugh. "And it's probably out of your price range at five dollars."

"Aye, then," I said in my best Irish accent. "Perhaps a little arm wrestle for the tab would be in order, then?"

Now most of the locals at the bar looked up with interest.

"You're on, chum. And a round for my mates," Paddy said, rolling up his right sleeve. "Double or nothing."

"That's fair," I responded, winking at the blokes and placing my right elbow on the bar.

Paddy put his down and grasped my hand. I noticed his wasn't as fleshy as mine. We gripped each other tightly and the local with the flatulence said, "Okay, on the count of three. One, two —" On three, he cut wind again and Paddy and I strained to garner position.

The big Irishman smiled at me and started counting down like he worked at NASA. "Pin minus five, four, three, two, one."

My arm suddenly flew back and my knuckles almost embedded into the wood of the bar with a thud. The bar birds shouted out like they'd won the Irish Sweepstakes.

Paddy smiled and let go. "I'll give you credit, copper. You got balls."

I smiled back, flexed my fingers, and managed to pull out a 50. "Keep the change," I told him.

He poured me a dark stout and I nodded as I headed to the back of the bar.

Only one of the three pool tables was occupied, so I took my beer for a walk through the room off to the side that was filled with large-sized men with loud voices. I browsed the crowd as I strolled around, one hand casually in my pant pocket and the other occasionally hoisting my glass to toast an imaginary acquaintance. I kept away from the far corner, where a somewhat larger group surrounded a smiling Asian fellow who was probably the guest of honor. My deductive powers came to this conclusion due to his silly party hat and position under a balloon banner that read *Congratulations Leon — you poor SOB!*

I continued to work the room as I tried to place a face or overhear a name that I could latch onto. After a while, I sauntered out the door into the pool-table area. As luck would have it, I finally spotted someone recognizable, the big black dude that was noted on Bulloch's Vice list as Theodore Parker — affectionately known by his close friends and co-workers as Teddy Bear. He was racking up the balls on one of the tables with two other guys who looked vaguely familiar.

"Hey, boys," I said, as I picked out a cue. "Want to make a foursome?"

"Sure," said Parker. "I'm Ted."

He stretched out a hand the size of a baseball mitt and watched how mine was swallowed up by his as we shook.

"Jake," I said by way of introduction when he let me free.

He waved his cue stick at his two cronies. "These are my homies," he announced with a big grin.

The closest one extended a hand and I took it. "Hi, Jake. I'm Carl Ratinski."

So far so good. I'd been here only a short while and I had already met Teddy Bear and The Rat.

The other fellow did the same. "Hey, buddy. Doug Gilmour. These guys call me Happy."

"Ah," I said, taking his hand. "Like the movie?"

"You got it." He let go and took up a position at the far end of the table with the white cue ball.

Theodore Parker gently removed the black plastic triangle from the table and cried out loudly, "Happy, you gonna break my balls?"

Gilmour sneered, pumped his cue stick a couple of times. The cue ball struck the others like a gunshot. The balls spread widely across the table and we started taking turns. I noticed Teddy and Carl whispering to each other every time it was my turn. I tried to make some small talk.

"So, you guys work with Leon?" I asked.

"Nah, not directly," said Parker. "We're mostly Vice, but we cross over sometimes with Leon in Juvenile."

I remembered Laura telling me Leon worked Gang Enforcement and wondered if Teddy Bear was maybe testing me.

"I didn't know Juvie was connected with Gang," I said.

Parker looked casually over to Carl. "They intersect once in a while."

"What about you?" asked Gilmour. "You work Metro?"

"Nah, I'm not a cop," I admitted, figuring this was not a good place to be caught impersonating an officer. "Used to go to school with Leon."

"Ah."

Teddy and Carl were murmuring to each other again.

"You could have fooled me, though," said Happy. "You sure could pass for a cop."

"Yeah, I know," I said. "I get that a lot."

We continued on for another 20 minutes or so, setting them up, knocking them down, and feeling each other out.

"Want another round, Teddy Bear?" Gilmour asked.

"Sure," said Parker. He called out to Paddy, held up four fingers, and turned his hand around in a circle signaling the bartender.

The big Irishman showed up a minute later with four drinks. I noticed no money exchanged hands, which told me a lot about the vice boys and the bar.

"Not many girls here tonight," I pointed out, taking a sip of fresh beer. "You have many working in Vice?"

"A couple," Teddy answered.

"Yeah," Carl confirmed with a laugh. "They have their place. Like when we need a pussy to lure out some dog."

All three of them found that funny, so I joined in.

"Not good for much else, I suppose, right, Rat?" I said.

"Not really," said Ratinski with a sly smile. He hoisted his glass. "Here's to us dogs."

"Woof, woof."

I wiped some foam from my upper lip after taking a drink. "That reminds me, I thought I heard something about some vice cop broad getting her car shot at over the weekend?"

"Yeah, I heard somethin' about that," said Carl. "Bad news."

The other two nodded their heads forlornly in agreement.

"You guys know her?" I asked.

"Yeah, sure," Theodore Parker answered. "Why do you ask?"

I shrugged my shoulders. "I guess your division can be more danger-ous than others."

"It can be," said Carl Ratinski.

Gilmour was lining up a shot and when his shirt sleeve pulled back I noticed his watch and said, "But judging by Happy's Rolex, the pay is good."

Parker laughed heartily. "I can take you down the street and get you one of those knock-offs for $89, right, Dougie?"

Gilmour completed his shot and self-consciously pulled down his sleeve. "Yeah, sure."

"But," I pointed out, "that would be illegal."

The big Teddy Bear got serious for a second and whispered in an exag-gerated tone, "And no po-leece man is gonna do nuttin' against the law."

The other two watched me watching them.

"Of course not," I said, taking my turn to shoot. "But with everything you have to put up with, you guys, and girls I might add, deserve some kind of bonuses or freebies, here and there, no?"

"No," said Carl Ratinski sternly. "It would still be against the law."

"Still," I said, pocketing the nine-ball, "I'd be tempted."

With the end of the game and the direction of the conversation, the mood had turned cooler. This was broken by one of the guys in the recep-tion room who swung around the doorway and announced brightly, "Hey, Leon's fiancée just pulled in out back and is comin' in. We'll finally get a chance to see what she looks like!"

"Well, thanks for the game, fellas," I said. "It was fun."

"Sure thing," said Theodore Parker. "You got a business card or some-thin'? We could call you next time we're thinking of shooting. . . ."

I didn't like that phrasing.

"Damn," I stated, as I patted my pockets. "I'm all out. Why don't you give me one of yours, Ted?"

He studied my baby blues with his mean-looking browns. "You can find us here, Jake. We're usually down here playing after work."

"Sounds like a plan," I told him. "I'll look you guys up."

"You do that," said the big Teddy Bear.

From the doorway, somebody yelled, "She's here!"

Chapter

Everyone crowded close to the front of the room. A guy standing next to me told his buddy that nobody at work had ever seen Leon's fiancée. The back door opened and one of the cops held the door open for the new, about to be, Mrs. Tang.

The woman walked in like she owned the place, strutting right up to Leon and planting a wet one on his cheek. She had long curly red hair and was wearing hot pants and an almost sheer halter top. Poor Leon. His face had gone beet red. Fifty guys started to hoot and holler because she looked like some kind of hooker. I knew it was Laura.

"Attaboy, Leon!" somebody shouted.

Someone else called out, "Nice catch."

"How much an hour to get married?" yelled out yet another.

Billy came walking in just then and one of the guys said, "Ah, it's just Laura. She musta been on the job."

A round of groans circled the room.

"You guys are really funny," announced an embarrassed Leon.

"She still looks hot!" somebody up front called out.

"Keep your hands in your pants, boys," she yelled out. "You stiffs can't afford me."

Another round of groans echoed through the room.

I was standing there smiling and shaking my head when I saw Laura notice me near the back. She said something to Leon and gave him a quick peck on the cheek. A moment later, after fending off good-natured propositions from half the men she passed, she met up with me.

"Hey, sailor. Buy a lonely gal a drink?"

"Why not?" I said, and walked out to the bar with a number of envious eyes burning a hole through my back.

We got to the bar and Paddy came right over.

"Uh, no offense, lass, but no working girls allowed," he said to Laura and then looked at me. "Even to hard-luck cases like this one."

She smiled seductively, opened her purse, and flipped Paddy her badge. The big Irishman was duly impressed.

"I take my whiskey like I take my men — straight up," she told him. "And not the watered-down piss that you're probably serving to those drunks back there. Preferably Jameson or Bushmills."

"And your friend, another stout?"

Laura put an arm around me. "He takes his beer like he takes his women. Cold, wet, and as much head as possible."

"Another comedian." Paddy went off in search of our drinks.

"So what are you doing here?" I asked Laura.

"I was going to ask you the same thing."

"I just wanted to check out some of these guys you work with. See if I could pick up anything that had to do with what happened to the two of us in your car."

"You'd better be careful, Jake. These dogs bite."

"And what about you?" I asked.

"Just thought we'd drop in and play a joke on good old Leon. He's been telling everyone what an angel his future wife is."

"I have to admit. You had a few guys going in there."

Our drinks came and I started to search for some money.

"Don't bother," said Laura. "I've got it. I'll expense it."

"I'll drink to that," I told her. "Just don't arm wrestle Paddy for the round. I learned my lesson the hard way."

Laura looked up at the husky bartender. "Arm wrestle?"

Paddy seemed to blush. "But not with a lass, ma'am. Wouldn't be fair."

"Oh, come on," Laura insisted. "I'll try not to hurt you."

The Irishman went redder.

Laura persevered. "Double or nothing." She rested her right elbow on the bar.

Paddy looked around the bar in embarrassment. "I'll try not to break any of those pretty nails, and I promise not to bang your knuckles into the bar like I did with your friend."

She looked at me with mock disgust. "You wimp."

I took a drink of beer. "Fine," I told her. "Go ahead. See if I care. You're into pain anyway."

Laura picked up her shot glass, tapped it against my mug, and tossed the whiskey down in one gulp. "Ah," she said, making a face. "A fine blend. Make it another, Paddy my boy, and it's a bet."

Paddy roared in laughter and his mates along the bar chuckled in unison. "I'll give you the bloody bottle if you beat me."

He took Laura's hand in his and they slowly gripped each other.

I counted out. "One, two, and three!"

The two of them held fast as they measured each other up. Laura was biting into her bottom lip slightly and a couple of veins were popping out on her forehead and neck. Paddy didn't seem to know if he should yawn or have a drink, and he would let her get the upper hand for a few seconds before he would easily bring back his wrist.

"I don't want you to hurt yourself, lass," he told her. "You can just call out quits."

The boys along the bar chanted for him to finish her off.

"Look, sweetheart," Paddy said. "I'll let you save face. You can use two hands."

As far as I could see, Laura could use both hands and both feet and it wouldn't make a difference. The guy was just too strong.

"Two hands?" she asked, puffing slightly.

"Sure, doll." He winked at his friends. "Anyway you want to use them."

"I can use both hands, however I want," she restated.

"Yes, but hurry up," he told her. "I've got to get back to —"

Laura lifted her left hand off the edge of the bar, brought it across low in a karate-style chop, and hit Paddy on his resting right elbow. His arm flew out from under him and Laura smashed his knuckles hard into the bar. The sudden motion must have turned something in Paddy's shoulder, because he looked as if he couldn't decide what needed attention more.

The guys along the bar were shocked.

Paddy looked at Laura with derision.

She smiled and said, "You said I could use two hands, you big, dumb, Irish bastard."

I held my hands up to Paddy and shrugged my shoulders to show him that Laura was out of my control.

Laura flexed her fingers as she attempted to get back some of her circulation. "Trying to take advantage of a poor weakling," she said in a condescending tone.

"You're no damn weakling," he countered.

"I wasn't talking about me," she said. "I meant you picking on poor Jake here, earlier."

I frowned at Laura. "Thanks. . . ."

It looked as if she had bruised his ego as well as his arm. "You caught me off guard, little lady. It won't happen again. I'm always here for a rematch."

Laura walked around the bar and took the bottle of Jameson's off the shelf and poured herself another shot. She threw it back.

"Arm wrestling is for sissies," she said. "Big Irish sissies."

Now Paddy was biting down on his bottom lip.

I didn't like the direction this conversation was going at all. It was almost as if the two of them had something personal going on. It also made me wonder if it had anything to do with Teddy, The Rat, and Happy Gilmour.

"I had a no-holds-barred idea in mind," she finally told him.

Paddy's eyes widened and the stinky guy at the bar let one loose as if to highlight the invitation.

"You mean like a boxing match?" he asked incredulously.

"No, I mean like a full-blown, no rules, full-contact, ultimate-fighter event," she explained.

"You must be fucking joking," he laughed. "You're not even 10 stone!"

"No joke," she said gravely. "We'll go into the reception room. There's 50 to 60 guys back there who'll love to witness me kicking your fat Irish ass."

"Actually," I interrupted, "I think he's Polish. His name is Stanislov-kowski."

"Okay," she continued. "Big deal. I'll kick your fat Polack ass. You win, I get the drinks for the rest of the night for everybody, so you know they'll order until they're shit-faced. And if I win, it's a night on the house for all of them."

I could almost see the cogs working in his head trying to figure out what the trick was. While Laura poured herself another drink, Paddy looked at me, wondering if she was crazy. I shook my head forlornly and ran a finger across my throat trying to warn him off.

Finally, he shook his head and said, "Take your bottle and fuck off, both of ya."

Chapter

I escorted Laura over to an empty booth off in the corner before Theodore Parker spotted us or she got into a brawl with the bartender. When we were settled in, I told her a little more about my time spent playing pool with her strange co-workers and my concerns that this place was some kind of home turf for them.

"They're always here," Laura said, lighting up a cigarette.

She hadn't gotten off on any sex that I knew about, but I guessed that the confrontation with Paddy was close enough for her to warrant a smoke.

"I'm pretty sure," she said, "that they've got some protection thing going here. If I remember correctly, there was a time when most people wouldn't frequent the place because of the lowlife that were hanging out here."

I looked around to see if the boys were still back there, but I didn't see them.

"Makes you wonder if Teddy's guys are any better to have in your place," I said.

"Good point, Sherlock." She poured herself one more shot and slammed it home. "Yowser!"

"I hope you don't have to go back to work after all that Jameson."

Laura looked at her watch. "Yeah, I think we're going to do one more sweep. See if we can drag the bastard out."

I shook my head. "Well, be careful hustling in those heels. You'll probably be walking a little bit of a crooked line."

She leaned over and gave me a warm kiss on the lips. "I'll look even more of the part if I'm teetering and tottering, don't you think?"

"Yes, I'm sure you'll look great out there," I told her.

"What are you going to do?"

"I'll probably hang around here for another hour or so. See what else I can dig up."

Laura stubbed out her cigarette and had one more for the road. She took out a pen and wrote something on a business card.

"Here's my home address. It's around midnight now. Meet me there at two."

"Okay," I said. "Sounds like a plan."

She gave me another kiss, this one a little rougher. "Oh, you should see what I've got planned. You're going to be taking a ride on the Kinkyville Express."

I laughed and wrapped my arms across my chest. "Oh, no," I cried out in mock fright. "I don't know if my boobies can take any more kinky."

"And don't be late. Mistress Laura does not like to be kept waiting."

With that, she started to stroll off, but suddenly stopped and turned to the bar. She held up the bottle of whiskey and shouted out, "And thanks for the juice, Paddy, you big, ugly bastard."

I picked up my beer and walked back toward the party. I didn't bother saying a thing to the bartender, but subconsciously, I knew I was listening for the sound of a thrown glass or ashtray.

◆

I spent the next hour mixing in with those guests who were hanging out late. I caught sight again of Theodore Parker with his boys, as well as a couple of new faces. When our eyes met, there was no invitation to come over, just a cursory nod of the head. At one point when they weren't looking, I managed to take a couple of group shots with my camera phone. I pulled Lieutenant Oakley's business card from my wallet and e-mailed the pictures to him, asking if he or The Bull could identify the ones who were not in the package he had sent to me.

Not a lot of information gathering was being accomplished, so around 1 a.m. I decided to hit the road. I figured if I left now, I'd have time to catch a burger and some fries before heading over to Laura's. I hated being tortured on an empty stomach.

I didn't really want to say goodnight to Paddy, so I decided to leave via the back door. The Bugatti was parked in a lot behind the Nugget, and I could get to it through the alleyway behind O'Reilly's.

The air was hot and surprisingly humid back here. I figured that it couldn't circulate very well with all the buildings packed in so close to each other. The air was also foul smelling as this was where all the dumpsters were located for the food shops along the street. To make matters even worse, the further I got down the dark alley, the more I realized that this would be the perfect place to get mugged. Now I started to look behind me and around doorways as I walked. At the darkest point I heard a can skitter across the pavement and the shuffle of cardboard. This was extremely frustrating because I could see my car farther down across the road in the lit lot.

Without much thought, I went into police mode, pulled out my practically empty wallet, and held it up to my mouth like it was a walkie-talkie. I couldn't for the life of me remember all my old codes and alarm calls, but I doubted it would matter to a couple of crack heads or winos who might want to jump me.

"Central, this is Patrol," I announced in a loud, official tone. "I'm on a code seven with a possible 903. Over."

Shit! I thought. My nerves must have been on edge, because I just now remembered code seven was out of service to eat. The 903 I had pulled out of the air because it sounded good.

I heard the distinct muffle of voices, and someone say "A what?" followed by someone else saying, "Ssshh."

I thought about making a run for the street and the safety of my car. The Bugatti packed a beautiful old-fashioned tire iron just for these occasions.

"That's a copy, Central," I continued, scanning the alleyway and breathing hard. "I'm heavily armed for either a 10–91 or an 11–26. Officers Riggs and Murtaugh are backing me up. Over and out."

There was more shushing and suddenly a dark shadow emerged from a recessed doorway and was followed by another. I found them peculiar as they were both wearing ski masks in this heat.

"Hey, brother," called out shadow number one. "What are you doing back here? We've already got this location covered on a code five."

My heart rate dropped and I could clearly remember code five meant stakeout — uniform officers stay away. I let out a big sigh of relief and put my wallet away. Three more shadows emerged from the other side of the laneway.

"Wow, am I glad to see you guys. I was getting a little freaked out back here."

"Yeah," shadow two said. "We heard your codes. What the fuck was that all about?"

I managed a little laugh. "Just nerves, I guess."

"The Riggs and Murtaugh part was good," said one of the shadows on the other side. "Those guys are cool."

"Well, I'll let you boys get back to whatever it was you were doing," I said, and started to walk slowly forward.

Shadows one and two stepped out farther into the dark alley. "But you don't want to miss the 243 in progress, now, do ya?"

A couple of the other shadows had flanked me before I realized a 243 meant assault on a police officer. "Hey, guys, there's been some kind of mistake. I'm not a police officer for real."

Shadow one stepped back in shock. "You're shittin' me. Really?" He stepped a little closer. "Then we'll have to switch it to a 112, I guess — impersonating a police officer. Either way, you're fucked."

I put a shoulder down and drove forward. It felt like I was running a gauntlet as fists and heavy flashlights rained down on me. I was stopped by a thick body and my cheek was nailed with a roundhouse punch. As I fell to the ground seeking any kind of protection, I wrapped my arms across my face. Steel-toed shoes hammered at my shins, thighs, stomach, and rib cage, causing flashes of lightning behind my eyes.

The assault slowed for a second.

"You fucked up, my man."

I tried to catch my breath, but it felt like one of my ribs had broken. "You're not cops?" I wheezed. "Then just take my wallet for Chrissake."

"Oh, we is po-leece, that for sure," said a familiar voice. "But you told us you weren't."

I coughed up what felt like blood. *Damn*, I thought, that could mean the rib went through into my lung. "I'm not a cop. . . ."

"You got cop written all over you, asshole," somebody else shouted and kicked me in the stomach. "Plus you were rattling off codes."

"I was a cop," I managed to get out. "A long time ago. I'm not from around here."

"Well, you still fucked up, *Jake*. . . ."

I didn't want to let on I had figured out who they were. After all, they still had masks on and that could mean they weren't going to kill me. Otherwise, why wear them?

"I don't know what you guys are talking about. How do you know my name?"

A low chuckle came out from the familiar voice of Teddy Parker. "Even more important, crackerjack, how'd you know Carl's nick is *Rat?*"

Well, the cat was out of the bag. My head was spinning trying to remember reality from bullshit. "His name's Ratinski," I panted — slowly. I could barely talk at all. "I heard you guys call him Rat, that's all."

"*Beeeep!* Wrong answer, douche bag." A boot caught me in the back of the head. "We had a meetin' on that, and all of us agreed nobody used his nick. That's only for special occasions and things, anyway."

Now I couldn't remember if they had used the name or not, or even if I had. What had me about to piss my pants was that they knew that I knew who they were.

Somebody said, "Well, can we at least take off these fuckin' masks? Won't make much difference now. . . ."

"It will if anybody sees us leavin', numbnuts," said the voice in charge. "Leave 'em on. All of ya."

Well, so much for their non-identities being able to save my ass.

"I say we whack him now and stop fuckin' around," somebody offered.

"You know," said the boss, leaning down so I could hear. "At first I just thought you was some kind of cowboy with his nuts on fire for the Bulloch broad, 'cause it was plain as the black on my butt that you was pussy-whipped."

"Here, I'll fix that."

A shoe caught me square in the groin and the night seemed to light up with fireworks.

"Those in favor of poppin' him now?"

They might have thought of my life as some democratic vote, but I was still all for the old-fashioned judge and jury and time off for good behavior.

"Hey, guys, enough's enough. I promise, I'm outta here. Hell, I'm outta the state for that matter. I'll do whatever you say."

Anything to get me one more sunrise.

As I tried desperately to catch my breath, somebody called out, "Nighty, night. Sleep tight. Don't let the —"

Then I heard the thunder of a gunshot as something hard slapped into my skull.

Then I heard nothing, nothing at all.

Chapter

"Jake. *Jake!* Wake the fuck up!"

Last summer, when I heard God talking to me after I thought I had drowned, He had sounded very much like a tender, caring, Lieutenant Oakley. Now, after being shot in the head, He sounded an awful lot like an anxious, profane, Laura Bulloch. Then it dawned on me that maybe I hadn't made it up to the cloud section after dying.

Damn! I thought to myself. I knew I shouldn't have cheated on my Hail Marys as a teenager after confession. As if verifying this fact, I felt what seemed like a little pitchfork being jabbed into my arm by some imp from the fiery location.

"Wake up!"

I managed to crack one eye open, only to find Laura leaning over and prodding me with her long, sharp fingernails. My other eye followed the first.

"Laura . . . you're not the Devil," I croaked.

"Maybe not," she said. "But he and I are good friends."

I got up on one elbow, wincing at the pain that shot through my side, and looked around. We were alone. The side of my head was knocking like the engine of my old Chevy and I reached to check for the entry point of the bullet. The only thing I found was the start of a swell bruise.

Laura reached out an arm and helped me to my feet with a lot of effort. I tried not to cry out too much from the pummeling my body had taken.

I noticed she had changed from her street-working outfit and was now wearing a light top, sensible jeans, and sandals.

"Sheesh," she said. "Can't I leave you alone for even a few minutes without the crap getting beaten out of you?"

I stood gingerly as Laura held me for support. I felt worse than a Persian rug in a carpet-beating contest. I checked my jaw and front teeth.

"Yeah, but you should see the other guy," I told her.

"Right," she snorted. "My hero."

Laura put my arm around her shoulder. "Come on. Let's get you to your car. I don't want to get ambushed in here. Like some dumb shits I know."

We started down the alley toward the Nugget.

"What happened?" I asked her.

She hefted me higher. "Not now. Let's go get you fixed up first."

I didn't really have the energy to argue. As a matter of fact, I was so woozy I wasn't even sure I could follow much more than a short sentence with single-syllable words.

"Okay," I caved in. "You're the boss."

Laura quickly checked the street both ways as we exited the alley.

"You're fuckin' right about that," she concurred.

With Laura driving and having no problem with the stick shift of the Bugatti, we made it to her place in less than a half-hour. Her house was located in a pretty, modest subdivision on the southwest end of town, filled with people of moderate means with hopes of moving on up in the near future. Minivans seemed to be the choice of vehicle for almost every other driveway.

"You know," Laura said as we pulled into her double garage. "You're special."

I managed to work free of my seat belt with the least amount of discomfort. "Mom always told me so."

"No," she said. "I mean, I don't usually let guys see where I live if and when I decide to bring them home."

"Oh, really?" I asked, and tried to laugh. "What do you do? Knock them out?"

"No, I make 'em wear blindfolds."

"Ah, I see. . . ." The trouble with Laura was you never knew when she was kidding or not. Somehow I thought she was pulling my leg again.

Laura turned off the ignition.

"I lied to you," she said, looking over at me.

I *knew* she had been busting my balls with the blindfold thing.

"I thought so," I told her, as she exited the car and came around to open my door.

"Yes," she said, helping me up out of my seat. "I did knock one of them out."

♠

Twenty minutes later, I was sitting comfortably in my underwear, my clothes were being washed, a cloth full of ice was being held to my head, and there was more ice in the tumbler of gin and tonic I was tending to. The room looked like any other normal living room; there wasn't a whip or dildo in sight, and as far as I could tell, the recliner where I lounged didn't have any leather restraints or electrodes.

Laura finished wrapping my chest with some wide bandage and taped me up.

"Tight enough?"

"Not yet," I told her. "It's still my first drink."

"Very funny," she said. "I meant the chest dressing."

"I know. You did a terrific job. It's just a dull throb now. Where did you learn all that?"

"I was a nurse for a few years before I joined Metro," she explained, as she put away her equipment in a huge medical kit.

"Well, that sure came in handy," I said, pointing to the case with the red cross printed on it. "I'm glad you had it."

"Oh, it gets used," she said with a sly smile. "You never know what can happen around here. Cuts, bruises, minor electrocution . . . hell, I even have defibrillator paddles for the older guys in case they conk out on me."

"For you, or for them?"

"Watch it, Morgan," she told me, giving me the evil eye and trying not to laugh. "Speaking of which, have you ever been hit with a Taser?"

I just about spit my gin up through my nose.

"Don't tell me you have one, 'cause that's where I definitely draw the line," I stated. "I got hit once in a special monitored experiment when I was a rookie cop. Don't want to go through that again. It hurt like hell and I drooled like a baby for an hour."

Laura had a wicked smirk on her face. "You know, done right, with low voltage and at just the right sexual moment, I'll bet it could be extremely stimulating."

"Yeah, well," I said, holding out my empty glass, "we'll never find that out now, will we?"

She still had the smirk on her face when she said, "Here, let me get you a refill. Then I want to hear exactly what happened in that alley."

When Laura returned, she handed me my fresh drink along with a couple of pills.

"Here, take these," she said. "They're prescription muscle relaxants. Heavy duty. Should help take the edge off what you're feeling all over."

I thanked her and went through the entire sequence of events from when she left the bar and up until she woke me up and helped me to the car.

"What the hell were those codes you used?" she asked, as she searched through a bookcase. "Ah, here it is."

She sat down beside me with a black police text I remembered from the academy and started to flip through its pages.

"I didn't know what I was saying," I tried to explain. "It's been a few years since I had to use them."

"Never mind, which ones did you use?"

"What does it matter?" I said, trying to recollect. "I know I used a code seven with a possible 903, but then I remembered the code seven was for out of service to go eat. But that made sense, because I was on my way to get a burger."

"Yeah," she said, as she trailed a nail down a list on a page. "Jesus Christ! The 903 is a report of an aircraft crash! No wonder you had them talking to themselves in the dark. What were the other ones?"

"You know," I tried to reason. "I was a little nervous at the time." Finally, I admitted, "I also said that I was heavily armed for a possible 10–91 and an 11–26. What did I know? It sounded official."

"Yeah," she said, as she shook her head. "Except to a cop. Ah, here it is. . . ." And then she started to laugh.

I sipped on my drink and waited for her to stop.

Finally she said, "You told them you were heavily armed for a stray horse and searching for an abandoned bicycle?"

Even I had to laugh. "I what?"

"Seriously," she said and handed over the book. "Look."

I took the text and confirmed what she had said. "How weird is that?"

I closed the book, sipped some more G&T, and asked Laura for her side of the story.

"Billy and I got word that the perv we'd been looking for struck way up on The Strip a little while after we left O'Reilly's, so we decided to call it a night. Since it was only around 1 a.m., I went back to the cop shop to change and took a taxi back to the bar to see if I could catch up with you. I tried your cell phone to let you know, but it was busy.

"When I got there, the crowd was pretty thin. Nobody seemed to have seen you leave, so I thought I'd hike over to where you said you parked the car and see if you'd left. If you had, I was going to take a cab over to my place.

"So anyway, I got down to where the parking lot is across the street, and I heard somebody making a commotion. I looked around the corner and down the alley and there was a gang of guys beating up on some poor schmuck. I couldn't tell if they were heavily armed, so I wasn't going to go in there on my own. Instead, I fired a warning over their heads. A couple of them fired off a few shots at me, and they rolled two of those metal disposal containers across the alley and headed the other way. If it was Parker and the boys, they wouldn't have wanted to get trapped in there if the other uniforms showed up. It could blow their whole cover and cause a massive investigation into their affairs. No, if they come after me again, it's going to be somewhere where I'll least expect it. And someplace where there will be no witnesses."

"Oh, it was Teddy and his band of thieves," I told her. "I can guarantee you that."

"Don't worry," she said. "I've got a few tricks up my sleeves, too. You just go get some rest. I might wake you up later to make sure you don't have a concussion."

Laura took a comforter out of a closet and draped it over me. "In case you need it. The air conditioning can get a little cool at this time of night."

She went to a drawer of a bureau, came back with a revolver, and placed it on a table next to me. "Just in case," she whispered. "I'm going to check the perimeter of the house and lock up tight. If you need me, just call out. I'm a real light sleeper."

"Thanks," I said.

She bent over and kissed me lightly on the forehead.

"Oh, by the way. Don't be alarmed if you hear me moaning and groaning and making a racket in my bedroom later. It'll just be me taking care of the Denny's rain check you promised me."

As she walked to the wall switch and turned off the light, my eyes closed and I was out for the count.

Chapter

Thursday morning for me came early Thursday afternoon. I eased my aching body out of the recliner and tried out my muscles and limbs. Not so good. I felt like I had gone 10 rounds with Mike Tyson. And not the Tyson of today either, but the one before he turned into a carnivore, when he still fought like a real man.

I turned my neck left and right and was glad to see it still worked. The bandage around my chest was holding in whatever was busted, but I'd live. I detected the smell of fresh coffee and let its aroma guide me to the source.

The kitchen was small, neat, and efficient, much like the rest of the house, street, and subdivision. I used my detective skills to locate a mug and proceeded to top it off. The house was quiet except for a splashing noise coming from down the hall, so I went to investigate.

There appeared to be three bedrooms: one used as an office, one used as a guest room, and the last being the master, where the sound was coming from. The door was open, so I walked in. The watery noise was coming from an en suite bathroom, where Laura was obviously taking a shower. I thought about surprising her by jumping in unannounced, but my good judgment said she was probably packing at least two weapons in there with her, and I wasn't stupid enough to try a stunt like that. I'd already checked the doorway for trip wires when I entered.

Instead I decided to look around and get to know my new friend a little better. I also had a nagging desire to know what, and how much what, was in that envelope that Michael had passed to Laura in the restaurant. I'd already accepted that she might have a teeny-weeny graft problem herself, but I could judge the situation a lot better if I knew the amount.

I carefully and quietly opened a couple of drawers and prodded her lingerie and socks. My only surprise discovery was a plastic baggie with about an ounce of white powder in it and a couple of prescription bottles. I quickly opened the bag and tasted the contents: cocaine. The description of the pills surprised me even more: lithium and some long name that started with *z*.

I peeked into a small walk-in closet and did the same there, noticing a couple of gym bags secured by padlocks to the zippers and handles. I went back into the bedroom and spotted a large, pine box stenciled with building blocks that spelled out Toy Chest. *Yeah, right*, I thought. I could bet my next paycheck that there wouldn't be any Nerf balls or skipping ropes in there — real ropes, sure, and maybe a ball gag.

I walked over to a dresser and quickly went through the drawers without finding anything else incriminating. So far so good. On the top of the cabinet was a silver tray with a short railing around it. Lined up in no apparent order were a number of oddly shaped and wonderfully colored colognes and spray mist bottles. I had to smile. As rough and tough as Laura tried to be, she was still a woman who liked the finer feminine things in life. I held a couple of them up to my nose to gather the fragrances, surprised at the range of her choices. Some were floral and some were fruitier, while at the other end there were a bunch that were woody and musky. My favorite was a round, yellow, eau de perfume right in the middle that had a bouquet scent subtly, yet strangely familiar. I wondered if perhaps my last love interest, Rachel, had worn it. On her, everything had smelled great.

Laura suddenly called out, and I froze. She carried on and I realized she had simply started to sing in the shower. I smiled again. I walked quietly over to the bathroom door to hear what song it was. My favorite shower tune was "Oh Susannah," an air banjo version I'd come up with, but Laura's turned out to be a much edgier selection of Springsteen's "Born to Run." As I left the room shaking my head, I recognized the song aptly fitted her.

I left the master and turned into the smaller bedroom that had been changed into an office. It contained a large pine desk, a green metal filing cabinet, and three wooden chairs, one on the business side and two out in front. I walked around the desk and began to open drawers. Each one contained the usual stuff: pens, paper clips, paper, and notebooks. In the bottom drawer I found a white envelope like the one I'd seen Laura accept at the restaurant. I pulled it out and examined the money inside.

There was about $2,000 in used 20s. More than just a free cup of coffee and the occasional meal. I returned the envelope to the drawer. There was a blank scratch pad on top of the desk, a few realtors' business cards, and a Rolodex. I scanned through the names and numbers, but nothing jumped out at me. I made sure everything was as I had found it and went back to the living room.

"Hey, there, sleepyhead."

I looked up from my magazine to find Laura dressed in a thick white robe. She rubbed her hair with a small blue towel and smiled across the room at me.

"Good morning, ma'am," I said, saluting her with my cup.

"I see you found the coffee."

"I was a detective, you know. And by the way, it is very good."

She came over and sat on a sofa next to me. "How are you feeling this morning?"

"You see this spot right here," I said, pointing to a small area behind my right knee. "Well, that's the only place I *don't* hurt."

"Ouch," she replied. "They really did a number on you. Are your ribs any better?"

"They hurt only when I breathe," I told her with a smile as I patted the bandage. "But seriously, thank you. You did a terrific job."

"Good."

There was a moment of silence between us, but I could tell there was something on her mind.

"So," she said. "Have you decided if you've had enough of playing good cops and bad cops?"

I laughed at the reference. "I've had enough of these guys shooting and beating the crap out of me. But that doesn't mean I'm going to roll over and die. If these boys think I'm just some flunky ex-cop with a crush on one of their own, well, they've got another thing coming. I'm just getting warmed up and I've got a few tricks of my own that I'm going to share with them. Cops from back East were nasty long before Las Vegas was a glint in Bugsy Siegel's eyes."

Laura looked at me solemnly. "Jake, this isn't your fight."

I shrugged my shoulder and winced. "They made it my fight."

She shook her head. "No. I don't want you to get involved anymore."

"Do I really have a lot of choice?" I asked. "They know who I am now. I don't want to have to be looking over my shoulder every time I walk out of my house."

"You're not going to have to," she said.

"What do you mean?"

Laura finished with the towel and placed it on the floor. She tucked her feet under her and hugged herself with both arms as if she were cold.

"I'm going to blow the whistle," she finally said.

I looked at her incredulously. "What? Are you kidding? You won't be able to walk down the street without endangering yourself! And Christ, nobody you work with will give you the time of day. You'll be an outcast."

"No, I won't. I'm going to testify to everything I know, then I'm going to say goodbye to Metro."

"You're going to quit? Give up everything you've worked for? Just like that? And for those assholes?"

"Jake, what do you want me to do? Fight it out with these guys for the rest of my career? And what about you? Am I going to have to worry about everyone I let into my life? No. That's bullshit. And to tell you the truth, this job is bullshit, too. I'm planning on doing whatever I can do to put these pricks away, or at least ruin their lives. Then I can get on with living mine. On my terms, not theirs."

I knew what she was saying, but I was trying to think of another way of solving the problem.

"Look, my uncle is retiring and there's nothing for me to stay for. I'm going to serve Parker and his boys up on a platter for The Bull and give him a nice going-away present."

"But what will you do?" I asked.

"Probably take some time off. Do a few things I've always wanted to do. I've got a few bucks saved, and I can always go back to nursing. Or, who knows? Maybe I'll try something right out of left field. Do something I really like."

It didn't appear that anything I said was going to make much difference.

"You could always open up an exclusive s&m parlor," I suggested.

"There's always that."

Laura got up from the sofa. "Your clothes are hanging in the laundry room. I don't want to be rude, but I've got some things to do this afternoon."

"No problem," I said. "Do you need a ride?"

"I'm okay. As a matter of fact, the insurance company is sending a taxi over so I can pick up my rental."

"About time." I got up out of the chair. "I'll get my clothes and find my way out."

Laura stopped me. "So you understand why I have to do this?"

"I understand what you're saying," I told her. "I just don't think I agree with it."

"But Jake," she argued. "You went through something like this and you ran."

"Maybe that's what makes it so hard for me right now. I'm tired of being the one who has to run away."

Chapter JACK JACK

There wasn't a whole lot I felt like doing after I left Laura's. I had some thoughts about what she was thinking of doing and also about what she had been involved in. I was still uncertain of where the graft from the restaurant put her in the whole scheme of things. Not only that, but something about the turnaround in her character didn't sit right with me. Granted, I didn't know her as a person that well, but I knew her type. And her type didn't run scared.

I went back to my place with a takeout order from Arby's and sat and watched Jerry Springer while I ate. It hurt to watch. After the second redneck couple started throwing fists, I switched the set off and finished my meal in peace.

I called the Oasis to check in with McClusky. He said there was no need to hurry back to work. Julius Contini had instructed him to give me a week off with pay for what happened with the murder of Mrs. K. That gave me until the end of the weekend and I was pretty sure I'd be a lot better by then.

The next thing I did was put a call in to Oakley. Regardless of what was going on with Laura Bulloch and me, I wanted to keep the lieutenant in the loop. If I had learned anything from my experience as a cop, it was to always have backup. I also wanted to know if he had any information on the other faces I had sent him by phone. He said he did and for me to come down to his office right away. I took a couple of Tylenol 3s and headed out the door.

♦

"Take a seat."

Lieutenant Oakley had his back to me as he keyed on an old-fashioned Remington typewriter that backed up the extensive array of computer equipment on his desk. He finished punching keys, tugged a form out, and held it up for inspection.

"I've got an eight-track player that might interest you," I told him.

"Laugh if you want," he said as he filed the document in his Out tray. "But it doesn't go down as often as all this fancy new hardware. And the only 'bug' I ever had was a dead fly that got squished in between the rollers one day."

When he looked up at me his eyes widened. "Jesus. Did Laura beat the crap out of you again? You look stiffer than some of the toe tags I've seen in the morgue."

I explained what had happened in the alley behind O'Reilly's and how Laura had intervened. I left out the shooting part as 'shots fired' were not taken lightly by Metro.

"What the hell were you doing there in the first place?" he shouted. "You don't even know Leon Tang."

"I was trying to get a line on the guys Laura worked with. See what they're like. See what they're working with."

"Well, judging by the bruises on your face and that lump on the left side of your head, I'd say they were working with a baton, a lead pipe, and a size 14 boot."

"Six pairs of boots, actually."

"This is worse than I thought, but don't say I didn't warn you. . . ."

He searched around his desk and found a manila folder marked "Morgan." When he opened it, two photographs slipped out. He removed a sheet of paper from the file and studied it. I noticed he also had a packet similar to the one that The Bull had sent to my house. Oakley turned the prints toward me and pointed the tip of the pen at one of the men. The photos had numbers circled above each of the heads. What really got my attention was that I had inadvertently caught one of them passing off an envelope to one of the new faces.

"Bulloch wasn't in this morning, but I have the list he gave you and did a little digging myself. These three guys," he said, tapping each of their heads, "have never worked the Vice squad. The closest one to Vice, this one," he said, pointing to number five, "is in Narco. This guy here, number six, is in Auto Theft."

"What about this guy here?" I said, indicating number four. "He doesn't even look like a cop."

"That's an interesting one, actually. He's a property officer."

"Case evidence, trace evidence, confiscated property?"

"Yup."

We both sat there with the cogs clicking in our brains.

"Are you thinking what I'm thinking?" Oakley finally asked.

"I've got a feeling that I might be," I said. "What an interesting mix to have operating together if you were all working against the system."

"Uh-huh. There's a lot of diversification between them that could come in handy and make them extremely versatile."

"Incredible when you think of all the fingers, and all of the pies."

"You know, as much as I appreciate what you're trying to do for Laura," he said thoughtfully, "this might be even more reason for you to stop sticking your nose in their business."

"You haven't heard the half of it," I told him.

I went on to tell him of Laura's decision to go to Internal Affairs and leave the force. His face went red.

"Those bastards are ruining a great career!" he thundered. "And her uncle will be devastated."

"She said this will be her retirement gift to him. Let it be part of his legacy. And judging from how she sounded, I think she's burnt-out. Wants to make a change."

It wasn't entirely true, but I was keeping my personal thoughts of her to myself.

"Well, all I can tell you is that The Bull will not go along with this. He'll take down the bad asses with her help, of that I'm sure. But let her quit . . . I don't think so. He'll work something out."

"That would be great if he could," I agreed.

We sat there for a while bouncing scenarios off each other and discussing the implication of Laura testifying against her squad. The repercussions were what really had us worried.

During this deliberation, the lieutenant was interrupted by the intercom. Although he had left instructions not to be disturbed, the desk sergeant insisted it was urgent and should be taken.

"It never fails," sighed the big cop, as he punched in a line on his console. "Oakley here," he said.

I couldn't tell what was being said, but his face was painting a picture of at least a thousand words. His eyes squinted, his brow rose, and his forehead frowned all in unison. A tiny vein on his temple pulsed in time with the thick carotid artery on his neck.

"You're shittin' me," he said.

Now I knew it was serious because he didn't often swear.

"If you're fuckin' around, I swear to God. . . ." He took a deep breath.

"Okay, I'll be right out there. Oh, and Paul, let's keep this to ourselves right now."

Oakley had collected himself enough that he didn't slam down the phone. He looked at me and said, "That was Detective O'Connor. Remember the one who interrogated you at the Oasis?"

"A real sweetheart. How could I forget him?"

"Well, they caught somebody trying to cash that $5,000 chip that went missing from Mrs. Kobayashi's suite."

I slapped the desktop with the palm of my hand. "That's great! I told you earlier: find the chip and you find your killer!"

Oakley wasn't sharing the same enthusiasm as I was.

"I hope not," he said solemnly.

"Why?"

He stood up, went to the coat tree in the corner, and put on his sports jacket.

"Because the person they caught trying to cash the chip was The Bull."

Chapter

Oakley said I might as well go with him since I was a so-called witness in the case, and we took his car. The trip to the Oasis was almost void of conversation as we tried to comprehend the impact of what we had just learned.

We left the car out in front of the casino and walked directly to the main cashier. The cage with the main vault was located in the most secure area of the floor plan. Besides all the security, there was a holding cell for occasions just like this. I was told to wait in the adjoining room with the two-way mirror along with my pal, Detective O'Connor, to verify whatever Bulloch might say about what had happened upstairs. The head of Security, a big burly fellow named Jim Kirk, was instructed to make sure everything was video- and audio-taped.

When Oakley entered the room, Captain Bulloch jumped from his chair.

"Jesus Christ!" he cried out as he went over and shook hands with the lieutenant. "Am I glad to see you!"

"Me, too, Alex, but you've gotta take a seat. I need to take a statement."

Bulloch looked astonished. "A statement? For what?"

His good friend could barely look him in the eyes. "Sit down, Bull."

"I don't understand. . ." he said in a hoarse voice as he sat.

Oakley glanced down at the table. "Look, Alex, I have to read you your rights, then we can discuss this."

Bulloch's eyes went wide. "Read me my rights!" he bellowed. "What are you talkin' about?"

The lieutenant looked up at him. "I read this, then I explain."

In the time it took Oakley to recite the Miranda, Alexander Bulloch seemed to age 20 years. His body collapsed within itself and the color drained from his face.

"What the hell do I need a lawyer for?"

Lieutenant Oakley went through the usual opening questions but kept things as light and friendly as he could under the circumstances. He was obviously not convinced that his old friend had anything to do with the murder of Mrs. K. and was giving him the benefit of the doubt. Still, he had his job to do and everything was being recorded.

"Where did you get the $5,000 Oasis casino chip, Alex?"

"I found it."

Security Chief Kirk and I exchanged glances.

"You found it?"

"Yeah, on my sidewalk. Why? Is that a crime?"

"Are you familiar with the murder of Mrs. Kobayashi that occurred here at the hotel last week?"

"That rich Japanese woman? Yeah, I read about it."

"Well, there was a piece of evidence missing when Homicide arrived."

Bulloch shook his head. "What the hell does that have to do with me?"

Oakley looked at his friend sorrowfully. "The missing evidence was a $5,000 Oasis casino chip."

You could almost see The Bull's mind assimilating the information and then seeing the connection. A semi-smile crossed his face. "Yeah," he countered. "But that's not the only $5,000 Oasis chip in circulation."

"That's the problem, Bull," Oakley stated. "Because of the recent tightening of homeland security, the high-denomination casino currency is microchipped nowadays."

Bulloch studied Oakley's face and eventually crossed his arms across his chest.

"I think I need that lawyer now, buddy."

"This is inconceivable!"

Laura and I were sitting at the Sidelines Sports Bar in The Palms Hotel sipping giant pina coladas. I had called her from the Oasis to break the news before she could hear the rumblings turn into roars through Metro.

"There has to be some kind of mistake," she continued. "Did he even know this woman? And wasn't she some kind of high-rolling, rich Jap broad? How would he ever come in contact with someone like that?"

I didn't want to explain *my* short-lived relationship with Mrs. K., let alone speculate what her uncle's might be, so I just shrugged my shoulders.

Laura shook her head. "The other thing I don't understand is what this has to do with a casino chip."

I told her how it was part of missing evidence from the crime scene.

"This is ridiculous," Laura said, as she stubbed out her umpteenth cigarette. "There has to be more to it. Some kind of explanation."

"I'm sure there is," I said, trying to console her. "Oakley's a good cop. He'll get to the bottom of it."

We sat and drank and commiserated for the next 20 minutes or so, and then my phone rang. It was Oakley. I told him where I was, what I was doing, and who I was doing it with. After that I listened to what he had to say. He hung up before I could reply.

"Oakley wants us downtown first thing tomorrow morning. He says, considering the situation, you've been given a temporary leave of absence and shouldn't worry about going in for your shift tonight. He also said not to worry too much, that there's a lot that has to be checked out before he will believe your uncle had anything to do with this case."

Laura fired up another smoke. She sat there forlornly, looking out over the cast of characters milling about the casino.

"I can't afford to lose my uncle, too," she finally said.

"Nobody's going to lose anybody," I assured her. "Let's go take it easy. Things should be a lot clearer by morning."

She nodded. "Will you stay with me tonight? At my place? I don't feel like doing much cooking, but we could order in."

"Sure," I agreed. "Why don't you head home. I'll stop and get a few things from my place and meet you there in a couple of hours."

With that, she got up, leaned over, and gave me a kiss goodbye. "Okay, I'll see you."

I didn't leave just then. The waitress came by and I ordered a beer. I wanted to think by myself for a little while about what had transpired. The news about The Bull was overwhelming. Why would a career cop be doing high-end jewel robberies? Sure, he might not be pulling in the same bucks as the squad members who were on the take, but would he resort to murder? I sat there contemplating the ifs and what-ifs. Having been a cop, I had heard all kinds of incomprehensible situations regarding the human psyche. There really didn't seem to be any limit to what one human being could do to another, or to themselves. Here was a guy about to celebrate an illustrious and decorated 20-something-year campaign as a community leader in a jail holding tank.

As a gambler, I was all too familiar with the pitfalls of greed. However, today's society was based on greed. Just look at the number of CEOs who were residing in their 6x10 suites at the Hoosegow Hotel.

When is enough enough? I thought. Then I remembered all the times I had been up all kinds of money playing poker and pissed it all back because I wanted to win more.

That made me mad and sad, so I went to the bar, ordered one more beer, and dropped $120 into the video poker machine trying to win back my good thoughts.

Yup. Greed kills.

I made it to Laura's by seven and the two of us spent the evening nibbling on Chinese food and imbibing the nectar of the gods. The conversation wasn't reserved, but it was hardly celebratory. We spent very little time analyzing the rationale and reason for someone like Alexander Bulloch to actually be responsible for what he was being held for. Instead, the majority of discussion was how he could have come in contact with the evidence. In a murder investigation, a coincidence like finding a casino chip on your walkway was highly irregular and virtually implausible.

So, in the end, we came to the conclusion that he either had to be guilty or set up. His guilt was extremely questionable, but could not be ruled out for certain without further investigation. If he had been set up, who was responsible? A motive, means, and opportunity would have to be proven for someone nameless, and how the hell do you do that?

Unfortunately, regardless of the explanation, Captain Alexander Bulloch now had an enormous hill to climb in order to collect his retirement benefits.

We both hit the wall about the same time and decided to leave the dishes for the morning. My sides were still tender, so despite the enticing thoughts of what could be in store for me in Laura's boudoir, I decided to spend one more night recuperating in the recliner.

♠

Laura and I arrived at the Clark County Detention Center on South Casino around 10:30 Friday morning. We were told at Reception that Lieutenant Oakley was expecting us on the second floor in Room 211 and that was exactly where we found him.

"It's not good," he told us when we had taken our seats.

Laura and I looked at each other, acknowledging that, right from the get-go, this was already heading down the wrong path. We waited for the lieutenant to continue.

"There was a team at The Bull's place all last night."

"And?" asked Laura.

Oakley let out a large sigh. "They found a few things that tie Alex to the murder at the Oasis. And maybe some things that lead him to a few other ones."

"What?" both Laura and I cried out in unison.

"I know, I know. Let me start from the one end for now. The Kobayashi murder. First of all, we found some seriously incriminating evidence while searching his house. If you remember, there was another murder at the Oasis that night: the room service kid. He was found with his throat cut and the knife was left at the scene. A fancy hunting knife.

"Well, they found a knife collector's box at The Bull's place, a matching set of three hunting knives of similar style in different sizes. Except the middle one was missing from the box."

Oakley stopped and studied our faces.

I spoke up first. "And the one at the scene is a perfect match."

"Yup," replied the lieutenant. "Right down to the maker's insignia on the blade."

Laura shook her head. "This is bullshit. . . ."

Oakley continued. "And you know the evidence tapes we pulled from Oasis Security?"

"The ones showing the suspect entering and leaving the hotel?" I asked.

"Well, they found a jacket and baseball cap in his closet that match the ones on those tapes."

I looked over at Laura. You could almost see that she was thinking it could all be a coincidence.

"They found traces of blood on the left sleeve," Oakley said. "From where the suspect could have held the victim's head while he cut him with the other. The lab is analyzing the traces and comparing them to the vic's blood type. Should hear anytime."

The three of us sat there for a moment in silence as the impact of what this evidence meant hit us.

"What about what you said earlier?" I said to Oakley. "About other murders."

"That's the real scary part. The investigators found a box filled with odds and ends of personal items not belonging to The Bull. Things like hairbrushes, cheap costume jewelry, ties."

"So what?" asked Laura.

"There were a bunch of photographs bundled up in a rubber band."

"Again, so what?"

"They were photos of persons recently killed. We think most of them were the cases we've had over the past year. Ones similar to the Kobayashi murder and robbery."

"So," I said. "You're saying The Bull was involved in a murder for profit and/or murder for hire? A hit man?"

"I haven't said anything yet. I'm not sure myself. But the photos bother me. That's something a professional hit man would do for proof of a job completed. I'll be a lot surer about this whole thing when I hear back from the lab."

"This is unbelievable," whispered Laura.

"And the casino chip?" I asked.

"Alex still maintains he found it on the sidewalk going to his car. He said the thought of turning it in crossed his mind, but he figured somebody else would just claim the money. And since he was retiring, he could probably use the money more than somebody who would probably end up just gambling it away. He says he didn't do anything wrong."

I agreed. "He didn't if that's the way it happened. But it won't mean a thing if the other evidence is linked to him."

Laura was unusually quiet and reserved, although I could understand, all things considered. The shock had really knocked the wind from her sails.

Lieutenant Oakley looked at the two of us. "I know it sounds like I'm building a case against Alex, but I'm just giving you what I've been told. He's a good friend of mine and I'll do everything in my power to help him."

The phone on the desk rang and the lieutenant answered.

"Oakley here . . . yeah, uh-huh . . . goddamn it . . . yeah, later."

He replaced the handset.

"That was the lab. The blood on the jacket in Alex's closet matched the victim's."

Chapter

By noon Laura and I left the detention center and she asked me to drop her off at her place. Oakley said he would do his best to try to let Laura see her uncle between 8:00 and 8:30 in the evening.

"Meet me at Michael's restaurant around six, Jake?" she asked, about to exit the Bugatti. "We can have dinner and then I'll go see Uncle Alex."

"Six o'clock it is. But no salad," I told her, trying to pick up her spirits. "I'm having a steak all to myself this time. Nobody's leftovers."

The corners of her mouth lifted slightly. "Thanks for being here for me, Jake."

I just nodded and she closed her door and was gone.

I spent the rest of Friday afternoon sitting in the Sports Book at The Mirage. I was sharing a table with a rumpled copy of the *Daily Racing Form* and betting my next paycheck on colorfully attired little men riding four-legged animals counter-clockwise around a racetrack.

In between races I spent time thinking about Captain Alexander Bulloch. By the seventh race, I had come to the only logical conclusion for his situation: he was fucked. No matter how much Laura wanted to believe in his innocence, the severity and reality of the evidence were pretty damn convincing. As far as what made a guy of his position and stature into a savage robbing killer, I'd have to leave that to more analytical minds than mine. My brain was more accustomed to assimilating poker odds and determining if I was drawing dead against an opponent.

I left the equine extravaganza around five and went back to my place to clean up and change clothes. I checked my e-mail and deleted the ads for Viagra and penile enhancements. I was glad to see the photo of the Vice squad I had taken for Oakley at O'Reilly's had come through when I had carbon-copied myself. I printed a copy to keep on hand.

♦

The parking lot at Michael's was almost full. The maître d' escorted me to Laura's private corner booth in the crowded restaurant. I gave her a kiss and caught the wonderful scent of her perfume.

For a second, I was startled at its familiarity. I *knew* that bouquet. Although it reminded me of the favorite one I had smelled from the samples in Laura's bedroom the other day, on an actual person the recollection of the fragrance was much stronger, much more memorable.

"My God," I said. "That cologne you're wearing. . . ."

"You like?"

"It's absolutely scrumptious," I confessed. "And it's doing strange things to me. What's it called?"

"Jake, what an animal you are!" she exclaimed. "Actually, I can't remember the name. It's just something I picked up."

I handed her a rose I had plucked from the floral arrangement near the cashier.

"Thank you, Jake. You're so sweet."

"Think nothing of it," I said as I slid in beside her.

"Okay, I won't, since I'm guessing you took it from that beautiful display beside the cash register on the way in."

I unfurled my napkin and placed it across my lap. "You'd make a good cop."

Laura laughed and pointed to an open bottle of wine. "Help yourself."

I did as I was told. A waiter came by and took our order, then I held my glass up to Laura's.

"May bad fortune follow you all your days," I toasted. "And never catch up with you."

She tapped the edge of her glass against mine. "Amen."

We spent the next 15 minutes making small talk, almost as if we were trying to avoid discussing the trouble her uncle was in. Eventually, there was a lull in the conversation, and Laura broached the subject first.

"I still can't believe what they're saying about Uncle Alex."

"I know . . . it's hard, but. . . ."

"But we have to face the facts, right?"

"It doesn't look good, Laura."

Her eyes had welled up. "I know, but it doesn't make any sense."

"Some things never do, sweetheart."

Our dinner came and I tried to steer the dialogue in a different direction.

"No word from our buddy Parker and his boys?" I asked.

"I haven't seen hide nor hair of any of them. I don't even think they knew that it was me in the alley. If they did, they might have had it out right there and then and taken the chance that they'd get me before any uniforms showed up."

"Well, I'm glad for that, because that would mean I'd be gone to that big casino in the sky."

We talked for a while about the Vice squad and how she was going to take them down as soon as things were settled with her uncle. It seemed to pick up her spirits.

Eventually, Laura glanced at her watch. "I'd better be going."

"Good luck," I told her.

She pulled a 20 from her purse and placed it on the table. "Do you mind making sure the waiter gets his tip?"

"No problem," I said. "Since everything else is on the house, I might hang around and have a cognac."

Laura smiled. "That's my Jake."

She slid close and gave me a hug. My face was buried in her hair and neck, but I didn't mind one bit. The favorite flower fragrance she wore was making my head spin.

"Thanks for being here for me."

"No place I'd rather be."

She pulled away and gave me a kiss.

"Are you doing anything tomorrow?" she asked.

"Didn't have anything planned."

"I'd like to get away from all the bullshit. How about a picnic? Over at Lake Mead."

"A picnic sounds nice."

"Great," she said as she exited the booth. "You bring the wine and some cold beer. I'll bring the rest."

"Should be fun."

"Should be?" she asked with a saucy smile and then leaned over and whispered, "Maybe we can find a nice secluded spot. I've gathered up a lot of sexual tension in the last 24 hours that needs a major release."

"I'm your man, ma'am."

Laura seemed to like that. "Pick me up at 10."

I told her I would and watched as she left for the exit. The waiter came by, I gave him the 20, and I asked him for a Remy Martin VSOP. He seemed pleased with my choice and hurried off.

I sat there thinking about Laura and how my life had changed since I met her. My mind went over all the crazy things we had been involved in together in the short time I had known her: the punch-up at the retirement party, the car chase, the machine-gun fire, my first s&m session, the arm wrestle with Paddy, and my get-together with Parker and friends in the alley behind O'Reilly's.

And still, while I thought about all this, the familiar scent of Laura's perfume lingered. My brain seemed to be shouting at me. The unsettling part of it was that my stomach had tied up in knots. This was not usually a good thing. In the past, my gut instincts were something I respected and paid attention to. I had never been led astray by them before.

It had something to do with the perfume, I was sure of it. Where had I smelled it before? It couldn't have been somebody in passing or at the card table. No, this aroma meant something to me. Something very strong. Someone very special.

And then it hit me.

Jesus Christ! I almost shouted out.

I got up from the table and started for the door. As I did, the waiter came by with a silver tray.

"Sir?" he said. "Your cognac?"

I stopped, took the snifter, and poured it back unceremoniously.

"Gotta run," I explained.

And boy oh boy, did I ever.

Chapter

I parked down the street from Laura's house. It was still a little light out for what I planned to do, but I couldn't worry about that now. Time was of the essence. I started to wrap a rag around my hand as I walked up her driveway and around to the side door. I gave one of the small panels of glass beside the door a quick backhand, reached in, and unlatched the deadbolt. I was in.

I went straight for the bedroom and over to the dresser. The various bottles of perfume were all lined up and I sorted through them until I found what I was looking for. I held the atomizer up to my nose and inhaled. There was no question that this was what Laura had been wearing. I placed the bottle face out in the middle of the tray, took out my camera phone, and made sure I got a good shot of the brand name of the perfume: *Sakiwai*. I had jokingly referred to it as Suzuki, back in Mrs. K.'s suite.

It was no joke now. I punched in Lieutenant Oakley's e-mail and fired it off. Then I got the hell out of there.

"Is Laura with you?"

"No," Oakley replied. "She just went in to see her uncle."

"Good. Did you get the picture I sent you?"

"I'm looking at it on my laptop right now," he said. "And I know from your file that your birthday is in the next couple of weeks. So is this some kind of hint?"

"Very funny. Now listen, this is important and we don't have a lot of time."

I told him the whole story about Mrs. K., her perfume, and my discovery of the same one at Laura's residence.

After a moment, the lieutenant finally spoke. "So you're saying that finding the same brand of cologne in both women's bedrooms is a really big coincidence?"

"I'm worried that it's a bigger coincidence than finding a $5,000 casino chip on your sidewalk."

"The killer was wearing a pair of Nikes and I've got a pair at home, too. So what? Are you trying to tell me that Laura might be involved in this investigation now?"

"I'm worried she might be. . . ."

"You're a freakin' nutcase, Morgan!"

"Look, hear me out," I pleaded. "There's no one alive that wants to have Laura come out of all this unscathed more than I do."

"But. . . ."

"But I'm telling you, you have to listen. There's something in my gut that's trying to tell me something."

"Your woman's intuition again?"

I was exasperated. "Laugh all you want — if I'm wrong. Just do me a favor. I am unequivocally, 100 percent positive that the perfume Mrs. K. was wearing is the same that Laura was wearing tonight. The night she was murdered, Kyoko told me the name of what she was wearing was a rare perfume from home called Sakiwai, just like on the picture I e-mailed you. She was definitely wearing it when she was killed."

"I'm thinking: coincidence," said Oakley.

"Will you at least give me the benefit of the doubt that I could tell that both of them were wearing the same perfume?"

"Okay, so you know your smells. Let's say I give you that. So what?"

"Do us both a favor. Go through the list of items inventoried from the murder scene that night. If the casino chip is so damn important, maybe this should be, too."

"There wasn't any hallucinogenic in that cologne you were sniffing, was there?"

"Lieutenant, come on. Can you really afford not to look into this?"

"I'm lookin', I'm lookin'," he said. I could hear files being opened and paper being shuffled. "But you know what this means if you're right, don't you?"

"Yeah," I said solemnly. "I've been thinking about that since I left the restaurant. Still, if I wasn't sure. . . ."

I could hear Oakley reading off articles of clothing and personal items. He went through hair brushes, combs, lipsticks, feminine hygiene products, and even toothpastes.

"No perfumes," I stated when he had finished. "Don't you find that strange?"

The lieutenant didn't say anything, which meant he was deep in thought.

"No jewelry, and no perfume. The gold and diamonds make sense. The robber was there for that. But why a cologne? Could it be robbery wasn't the prime motive, but murder was? And if that's the case, could a planned execution have been the intention all along instead of some random murder?"

"You know what you're implying," he said softly.

"And I *hate* what it entails," I told him. "But still, this has to be checked out."

"What exactly do you recommend?"

"Look, I detest myself for what I'm suggesting, but I'll never be able to spend another honest minute with Laura if these questions go unanswered. She already scares the hell out of me sometimes and I'm falling for her."

"You could come out of this with nothing and looking really stupid."

"It wouldn't be the first time, but here's what I want you to do."

I told him my plan.

"You're good with this?" Lieutenant Oakley asked. "Even though we've discussed the implications before?"

"It has to be done."

"Okay, it's your funeral."

"Call me on my cell as soon as she leaves."

♠

My phone rang 30 minutes later.

"Laura just left," Oakley advised.

"What did you tell her?"

"Just what you wanted me to. First off, I told her what a great perfume she was wearing, and she told me she'd have to wear it more often because of all the compliments she was getting."

"Good, so that seed was planted."

"Then we started talking about you. And as much as I can't believe it, or figure out why, I think she's falling for you. As long as I've known her, she has never gotten serious over any guy, but it looks like she's making an exception for you.

"I made it sound as if it was a slip of the tongue, but I also made a big point of how weird connections and coincidences can be in some situations. When she prodded me to explain, I told her how you had actually been up in the suite with Mrs. Kobayashi when the murder had taken place, I related the whole scenario of how you hid under the blankets through the entire ordeal."

"And her reaction?"

"At first, nothing. Her eyes went into dark mode and she just sat there staring. Then she said she wasn't feeling well and wanted to get home."

"Did you get a feel for anything?" I asked.

I could almost see Oakley nodding his head. "Laura was pissed at something. She was trying not to show it, but I'm Homicide, and I know body language."

"We got a reaction."

"I hope it was only that she couldn't stand you being with another woman and not because of what you're suggesting," the lieutenant said.

"I wish it were, but I don't see her being that sentimental."

Oakley got more serious. "If what you're implying is true, then we have to look at those tapes again."

"Yeah, but I don't think you'll get much from them except that it could very well have been a female, albeit a strong one. They're inconclusive."

"Well, I thought it was a crazy idea, but now you've got me wondering. It doesn't make any more sense than The Bull being the guilty party. In fact, it makes it even worse. Now, not only are we saying that Laura might have been the trigger person, we're also suggesting she set her uncle up for it."

"Son of a bitch."

"So now that you've let the cat out of the bag, you better hope it doesn't bite you on the ass."

"You're right," I agreed. "This thing is getting more and more bizarre. I'll really be up shit creek if this plan doesn't work out."

"The pieces are starting to fall in place. If she goes for the bait, then we have our shooter. It's not a pretty scenario, but it is what it is. I'll have your back, just the way you suggested."

"I'm picking her up at 10."

"I'll have my people in place by daybreak. We'll have undercover units near her home, en route, and around Lake Mead. You'll be covered six ways to Sunday."

"I better be. Because if that little filly gets a burr up her ass, she can be plenty dangerous."

"Don't worry," said Oakley.

I took a moment to collect my thoughts. "You know, I appreciate this."

"And if you're wrong about everything," he reminded me, "you're gonna find out how dangerous I can be. Because when I'm finished with you, you'll get a fat bill from County: double-time for every officer involved."

"I'm betting with my head this time, not my heart."

The big cop was silent for a moment. "Call me when you leave your place so we can wire you up."

Chapter

It was one of the most restless nights of my life. It came close to the night my police partner and lover, Karen, was knifed in an alley where I was supposed to be backing her up. I had screwed up there royally and would live with it forever. But this night was different. Although I was fighting for what I felt was right, I was experiencing flashes of doubt.

What if the coincidence of the perfume bottles was just that? Still, I reminded myself, that doesn't explain the missing inventory from Mrs. K.'s bedroom.

No. I realized I had put myself in a no-win situation as there was probably no turning back the pages in my relationship with Laura if I was wrong. I could never expect her to forgive me. No more than I could forgive myself for losing Karen.

By the time I did fall asleep, I was having serious doubts about Laura's involvement in such a vicious crime — all over a bottle of perfume that could have simply been given to her as a gift.

It was nine when I was ready to leave. I placed a call to Lieutenant Oakley.

"It's Jake."

"Everything is a go. We're already in place."

"Okay. I should be there in 15, 20 minutes."

"Good. Meet us as planned at the dark blue van in the little plaza at Livingston and Stanley. We'll fix you with a wire and run a test while you're driving to her place."

"Ten–4," I said, to make it official, and then I hung up.

Not knowing what the temperature or winds might be down by the lake, I threw on a light nylon jacket and tossed in my phone. My ribs were still sore and the piercing pain when I took a deep breath concerned me. I retrieved the bottle of wine and the six-pack of beer I had chilling in the fridge, and put them in a small cooler chest with a bag of ice. Then I locked up and headed to the garage.

It was a beautiful morning, slightly cool but filled with promise. There was no rainbow, or birds twittering like in the movies, but there was a definite feeling that the day was going to unfold according to plan. I just hoped I felt the same way by nightfall.

I entered the garage I leased for the Bugatti. As I opened the trunk and placed the beverages inside, a shadow walked past the windshield and someone called out.

"Good morning."

If the sound of a human voice could knock the wind out of you like a punch to the stomach, this one packed a wallop.

"Laura! What are you doing here?"

She came around back and hefted a large wicker basket into the trunk. Her outfit consisted of a loose-fitting denim shirt, basic jeans, and a pair of white sneakers. She was dressed for fun, but her demeanor was business-like and serious.

"Couldn't sleep. So I thought I'd save you the drive and come over here."

"Sweetie," I said. "You should have called me when you left the house."

"I left early."

I wondered if Lieutenant Oakley's people had picked up on that. I glanced nonchalantly out the garage to see if I could spot them.

"Really early?" I asked.

"Yeah," Laura said. "It was around four o'clock this morning."

"Four?" I said, astonished.

"Like I said. I couldn't sleep. With everything that's happened, I have so much on my mind right now."

"I guess I can't blame you," I told her, trying to stall for time and wondering how I could get a hold of Oakley to let him know.

"C'mon, let's go, Jake."

I snapped my fingers. "Give me a minute to run inside. Silly me, I forgot the corkscrew."

"Not to worry," she said. "I remembered to pack one in the basket."

"That's what I like about you," I told her. "You think of everything."

"I'm looking forward to today. It could be a defining moment in my life."

Now I wondered what she meant by that. Did it mean I was worrying about nothing and she was just working up the courage to admit that she was falling in love with me, or was she on to Oakley and me and I wouldn't make it alive into tomorrow?

"Me, too," I agreed.

I supposed that meeting with her uncle last night could have had her riled up so much that she couldn't sleep. If this whole thing with the perfume was a mix-up, she might even be a little reticent because she had learned I was hitting the sheets with someone else so soon before we had met. After all, women were known to get jealous from time to time.

Still, everything seemed a little too convenient right now, and my radar was fully tuned. I wondered if the male tarantula felt something like this just before the female killed him after lovemaking.

"Jake, it's such a beautiful day, do you mind if I drive?"

"Uh, sure. I guess."

I walked around to the passenger side and got in, scanning the street for the boys in blue. Except for the two kids tossing a Frisbee on the side lawn and the local dealer down on the corner selling rocks of crack to a taxi driver, the neighborhood was deserted.

Laura dropped the transmission into first and we slid out and down the driveway. We eventually got onto Flamingo and headed east toward Boulder Highway.

"You sure you got everything?" I asked casually. "We've got plenty of time before lunch to stop by your place."

"No, we're fine. I thought of everything."

Yeah, that was what had me worried.

"You know," I said in my bedroom voice. "We even have time for a frolic or two at your place."

"Mmm. Sounds delicious," she admitted. "But I'm feeling slightly raunchy and outdoorsy today. Besides, I've got something special planned."

I could tell changing her mind was hopeless. I'd have to go along for the ride. The last time I had felt this bleak was when I was a kid and my dad sent me up to the door of the Boston Hell's Angels clubhouse to trick-or-treat on Halloween. Turned out they gave out the coolest stuff — candy cigarettes, chocolate cigars, and little Harley motorcycle key chains with skull flashlights on the end. Hopefully today would turn out to be as unsuspectingly favorable.

We chatted as we drove, but when I brought up last night's visit to see her uncle and Oakley, she told me she just wanted to enjoy the drive and talk about all that "nasty" stuff later over a cold one.

Eventually Flamingo met Boulder Highway, and where I thought we were going to turn right and head south for the traditional route to Lake Mead, Laura went through the intersection and turned north on Nellis.

"I thought we were going to the lake for a picnic?" I asked innocently.

"We are," Laura answered. "We aren't in any hurry, so I thought we'd take the longer scenic drive along 147."

"You see. That's the other thing I like so much about you. You're always full of surprises."

"That's me," she admitted.

We drove for a while without saying any more. When Laura turned onto 147 and started heading east, I knew I better try to get a hold of Oakley somehow to let him know our plan was FUBAR. The rows of strip malls and houses had ended a few miles back and now we were passing the occasional trailer park and gun shop.

"We should probably stop for gas," I suggested.

Laura looked down at the fuel gauge. "You're right. I'd hate to get stuck alone out there without enough to get back."

"You mean the two of us, right?"

She looked at me with an odd facial expression. "Of course. Alone was just a figure of speech. Don't worry. I'll stop up ahead."

I tried not to act worried, yet couldn't help but nonchalantly glance back to see if we were being tailed.

"You okay?" Laura asked.

"Yeah," I told her. "My neck still has some kinks in it. I'm just trying to stretch them out."

A few minutes later, Laura pulled off at a lonely, no-name gas station on a corner of some desolate side road, and took the furthest pump away. I got ready to get out to try to call for help while I filled the tank.

"Don't bother," said Laura.

"It's no trouble."

"Jake," she said with a stern look as she took the keys from the ignition. "I insist."

She got out of the car and walked to the back of the Bugatti. I heard the clatter as she removed the hose, inserted the nozzle, and started to fill.

I looked back through the rear window and Laura waved back. What good was a cell phone if there was no way of calling without her seeing me? My mind began to race.

Suddenly, I had an idea.

I slipped the phone from my jacket and glanced down to check the settings. So far so good. I aimed the camera lens feature in the phone out the open window where the highway sign was and pushed the button. I slid my thumb over and pressed SEND. As I waited for the process to complete, I looked around for another shot. The sign over the station said Norton's Auto, so I made that my next. The photos, if Oakley got them, might be enough to lead him to our current position. The real problem was going to be finding us after we left here and ended up on some unmarked side road.

Laura finished up by putting back the hose and screwing on the fuel cap. Just then, a lanky, rumple-haired teenaged boy came running from around the building with two beagle pups tripping over each other in pursuit.

"Here Hansel!" he called. "Here Gretel!"

Even under the potential ominous circumstances, I found the fairy-tale names rather humorous. Then I found it constructive as it gave me a brainstorm. I remembered I had a few decks of used Oasis playing cards in the side pocket of the door beside me. I got a desperate idea and started to empty the packs onto the floor between my seat and the door. As I did, I pulled out the black aces and eights.

"Cool car," said the boy to Laura as he pulled up out of breath. "Sorry I didn't hear you drive in. I was out back feeding my new dogs."

"It was no problem," she said as she handed him some bills.

"I'll get you your change, ma'am."

"That's okay," Laura told him, bending over to ruffle both dogs' ears.

"Buy these two a nice lead so they don't run out here and get themselves into any harm."

"Gee, thanks," he shouted and ran off with the dogs following. "Come on, boy! Come on, girl!"

As Laura waved and went to get back in the car, I took two black aces and eights and dropped them on the oily pavement. Then I took the camera and took a picture of them lying there and sent it by e-mail. Hopefully, if Oakley picked up on this clue, he'd also pick up on the rest of the plan.

"Cute, huh?" she asked as we pulled out back onto the highway.

"For sure," I agreed. I palmed another set of aces and eights and inconspicuously tossed some more cards and sprinkled them like bread out the open window as we picked up speed. "I like dogs."

"Me, too. I'd like to get a pit bull to take care of my neighbor's poodle that keeps crappin' on my lawn."

"Yeah," I said, not wanting to make any waves. "Dogs are nice to have around."

We drove for another 20 minutes, the heat of the open desert getting warmer by the minute, and me palming and dropping more bunches of cards on the road as we went.

"I've never taken this route to the lake before," I noted.

"Yeah, it's kinda out of the way, but it's peaceful. Real quiet like. Don't get any semis and nosy tourists out here."

I didn't bother to remind her that we hadn't seen a single house, car, or person since we left the gas station.

"We'll be turning onto a shortcut side road in a couple of minutes," Laura advised me, "then it's a clear run to the lake."

"Sounds good," I said. "I'm dying for a brewski."

Laura kept a tight smile on her face and continued to study the road. About six or seven miles farther on, she leaned forward and took her foot off the accelerator.

"That looks like it," she said when we came upon a foot-high pyramid of stones off the shoulder of the pavement where a dirt road led off into the distance.

I reached for a big handful of cards and held my arm out the window. As she applied the brakes, and slowly started to turn, I let the cards fall from my hand slowly in as long a trail as possible. We made it 20 yards down the path when I finally ran out. I felt around beside me to try to determine how many more cards were left, anxious and disappointed to learn I was down to perhaps half of a deck. I had to hope there wouldn't be many more changes in direction to worry about.

"Actually, there's an old abandoned train stop from the late 1800s out this way. Do you mind if we stop there and check it out? If it's nice enough, maybe we can just have our picnic there."

I wasn't in favor of stopping anywhere, if the truth be known. I was happy right where I was, but under the circumstances, I didn't have a lot of choice.

"You're the boss," I told her.

Her smile rose. "Always."

We bounced around jauntily for a couple of miles following the worn path in the dry, cracked soil, as if the old Bugatti had been out in the middle of nowhere many times before. Then, when I remembered the history of the previous owner of the car, I realized it probably had been on numerous, fatal excursions where more passengers went out to the desert than came back. Hopefully this wouldn't be one of them.

Eventually some dilapidated forms took shape up ahead.

"I think that's it," Laura said.

As we neared, broken down images became clearer. Laura pulled up to the largest remains and stopped the car.

"Look at that," she exclaimed.

There wasn't much to see. It looked like the remnants of an old train stop, used, perhaps, more for cargo than for people. The largest of what was left of the buildings appeared to be a warehouse with a platform and ramp high enough for unloading goods. A wall here and there indicated where other structures had stood. The rusted-out tracks ended near a 30-foot water tower, or what was left of it.

Laura surveyed the area in every direction. "Imagine the history behind a place like this," she said. "Incredible."

To me the place looked sad and lonely, with a past that was almost certainly isolated, bleak, and where a lot of hopes and dreams had died. I was feeling anything but comfortable being here.

Laura went around to the back of the Bugatti and opened the trunk.

"Grab the cooler, Jake," she said, as she carried the picnic basket and started for the shade of the platform.

When we got there, she took a blanket out and spread it on the ground. I took out two cold beers and handed her one. We both cracked the caps and silently toasted each other before taking a drink.

"This is different," I noted, looking around.

"And no prying eyes," Laura suggested.

We sat for a moment in silence.

"So how was your uncle?" I finally asked.

Laura looked down and picked at the label on her bottle. "Not so good. He's really worried now with the introduction of the clothing and DNA evidence."

"But he still denies it?"

"Yes."

"And you had a chance to stop in and see Lieutenant Oakley?"

Laura looked across at me and nodded without saying a word. She drank slowly from her bottle, then she reached into the basket and pulled out a large, round, green tin cookie box with a painting of a jolly, red-cheeked Santa Claus on the lid.

"Yeah," she finally said. "We spent some time talking."

"He's a good cop. He'll find out if The Bull really had anything to do with that woman's murder. His record for closing cases is excellent."

"So I've heard," she acknowledged. "Which reminds me, I'll have to try to get more of that perfume you were so crazy about. Lieutenant Oakley was sniffing the air and commenting on it as well."

"Nice stuff," I told her. "Where did you get it?"

"That was the one I picked up in Japan," she said casually. "When I was out there last year attending the police conference."

Son of a bitch! I thought. I knew there could be an explanation for the bottle of Sakiwai. I felt like an idiot for going through with this little escapade to try to trap her. Now I had to hope Oakley didn't take it out on me and bill me for whatever manpower he had put in place.

And then, almost as an afterthought, Laura added, "Oh, he also told me how they kept your involvement with the Japanese woman out of the papers as well. I couldn't believe it. You were actually there when it happened?"

I looked up at her sheepishly. "Yeah, it's a long story."

"We've got all day, Johnny Stud. Go ahead, tell me."

I gave her a capsulated version, telling her how the meeting came about in the first place and leaving out the juicier details of our love-making.

"You dirty, dirty boy," she lectured. "So you weren't hiding in the suite somewhere, worried that it was her husband. You were actually in the bed the whole time?"

I may have blushed.

"So tell me," she said with a sly look about her. "What exactly were you doing under the covers, Jake?"

I hid the next blush by retrieving another beer.

Laura seemed to relax for the first time that day. You could almost see her body loosen up.

"So you didn't actually see anything, then?" she asked.

"Nope," I shrugged. "Not a thing."

"And all you heard were the shots?"

"Yeah," I told her. "That and the exchange in Japanese."

Her body went tight and acute once again. "You heard the killer speak? Did it sound like Uncle Alex?"

"They talked briefly," I said. "But I couldn't swear in court that it was The Bull. The voice was low and the words were softly spoken."

"So you didn't understand what they were saying?"

"No, all I heard was the shooter say something about a tissue and then *sayonara*."

"And they didn't work on you to see if you could remember anything else?"

"Not really," I said. "Maybe they'll try hypnosis or something if it comes down to that."

Laura dropped her head an inch or two, shook it sadly back and forth, and said, "Son of a bitch . . ." under her breath.

"What's the matter?" I asked.

She lifted her head and looked out over the silent, barren landscape.

"Unfortunately, you heard the wrong two words, buddy boy."

I smiled at her and asked, "What are you talking about?"

"You heard *teishu* and *sayonara*," she said sadly. "Actually, the complete phrase went something like *Anata no teishu ga sayonara to. Itsute Imas.*"

"Come to think of it, that sounds pretty close." I laughed lightly. "How the hell did you know that?"

"Easy," Laura said, as she got to her feet and pulled a small automatic pistol from underneath the back of her shirt. "It was me who said it."

Chapter

Now it was my turn. "Son of a bitch. . . ."

I literally didn't know whether to laugh or cry, so I decided on the most optimistic route, just in case. I started to laugh.

"You are one ball-bustin' broad," I said as I pointed my beer at her and began to stand. "You almost had me going."

She lifted her arm, and the crack of a shot rang out as the bottle exploded in my hand. I decided to sit back down and check that I still had four fingers and a thumb.

"What the hell are you doing?" I yelped as I wiped away shards of glass.

Laura began an agitated pace.

"I was afraid it might turn out like this," she said. "But I had to be certain."

"What are you talking about?"

"You and Oakley were having second thoughts about Uncle Alex's involvement. I thought so. After I got home last night and found my place broken into, I started to put some things together. Especially when I noticed that nothing was missing and that the only thing out of the ordinary was my perfume bottle that was out of its usual place. That made me note all the attention my cologne had been getting from you two lately. And since I knew where I had taken it from, that made me very nervous."

"So it was actually you . . ." I whispered, stunned.

"I spent an hour sitting there in the dark thinking and finally decided what had to be done. I never went to bed at all. Instead I prepared what I would need, then I parked my car down the street in the driveway of a vacant house around four in the morning just to be certain. Sure enough, at just about dawn, a couple of unmarked vehicles drove into the area and tried to look inconspicuous. I know a shadow net when I see one.

"I waited another half-hour or so and as I drove out of the subdivision and past a local plaza, I saw the Metro surveillance truck. That sealed the deal. I knew for sure that I was being set up. You were probably supposed to meet there and get wired for our picnic, right?"

I knew she didn't expect an answer. She already had it.

"From there I went to a cheesy motel and rented a room for a couple of days. That's where I'm going to say I've been all day today, worried about the break-in and too nervous to spend the night at my house. After that, I went to your place and waited. The fact that you were getting ready to leave so early also meant that I was right about you being wired.

"You know, Jake," she said sadly. "The thing is, if you hadn't admitted hearing anything . . . well, let's just say today would have had a better outcome for you."

"Heard what!" I exclaimed. "I heard some foreign words that had no meaning whatsoever."

"I can't take the chance, Jake. Especially if somehow you did manage to remember everything that was said. Unfortunately, you heard the only part that would lead the investigation away from the real purpose of that woman's death. *Teishu* and *sayonara* translate into *husband* and *goodbye*. How long do you think it would take someone to put two and two together and realize that the supposed bungled robbery and murder were really a carefully planned execution?"

My mind was reeling. "Are you telling me you were carrying out a hit?"

Laura shrugged her shoulders and sneered. "Sorry to burst your bubble, boyfriend. Shit happens. Mix one wealthy husband, worried about a wife who's threatening to ruin his empire, with somebody who can erase that problem — and you've got yourself a solution."

"That's insane."

"No, that's frontier justice."

My only chance now was to stall, keep her talking.

"Look, Laura, why don't we go back to town, get us a nice room —"

She swung her arm down at me and fired a shot into the dirt between the inside of my thighs.

"Shut the fuck up, Jake."

Laura went to the picnic basket and pulled out the last thing in the world I would have expected: a folding shovel, the kind from an army surplus store. She tossed it at my feet.

"Pick it up," she ordered as she moved back to keep some distance between us.

I did as I was told.

She pointed to the ground beneath the platform. "Dig a hole there about a foot wide and a foot deep."

I was pleased that it would be far too small for me to fit into and started excavating. When I was finished, Laura took the shovel and directed me off to the side. She took the cookie tin, opened the lid, and examined the contents. Even from where I was standing, I could see the bundled bills. She saw me watching.

"Common Las Vegas currency, Jake," she announced with a laugh. "One hundred thousand in unmarked hundred-dollar bills."

"Unusual bank security," I pointed out. "A Santa cookie tin and a hole in the ground."

"Unusual circumstances, my boy," Laura announced. "Payment for a job well done. I don't need to be caught with this in my possession. Unlike the others, this fee would be too hard to explain."

"The others?" I asked.

She looked like she was going to test out her aim once again. "Don't be so stupid and naïve, Jake. Did you think this was a one-off? They'll never be able to trace the other payments. They're all offshore now. Just like me in about two or three months."

Her face went sad for a moment. "Too bad you're gonna miss out on all those pina coladas and warm, white beaches. . . ."

Laura covered the tin, placed it in the hole, and filled it back again. She tamped the ground and spread the excess dirt.

"Okay," she declared. "Now it's your turn. Pick up the basket and cooler and let's you and me take a little walk over that dune."

Well, shit creek, here I come, I thought.

We walked about 50 yards until we came to the top of an embankment.

"Over the other side."

"Laura?" I protested. "Can't we at least talk about this?"

"Go," she ordered.

The earth was parched and cracked and I skittered down the 20 feet to the bottom.

"This'll do," Laura said. "Put the stuff down."

When I had, she tossed me the shovel.

"Dig."

"Laura, please," I begged. "You can't be serious."

Her face went livid and her complexion turned red. "Don't fuck with me, Jake! And don't treat me like an idiot. Because I am not. I have been told I am a lot of things, from a bipolar kid to a psychotic loner, but the one thing I am not is an idiot."

"But, Laura —"

"Look," she shouted. "You had your chance. And you know what? You actually amused me. For the most part, I hate men. But I thought that maybe you and I could make a go of it after I took down the squad. But you blew that. I can shoot you right now, but then I'd have to work on that hole in this heat. So why not just do as you're told? Dig."

I had to buy some time. I picked up the shovel and speared the ground. A shot of pain ran through my ribcage. The soil was dry gravel mostly and was going to take a little while. I struck again.

Laura walked to the cooler, retrieved a beer, and sat on the ice chest's lid.

The fact that she did not want to do the digging might mean I could get her to at least talk more and take her mind off my progress.

"The others," I said softly. "How many?"

She sat there, sipped her beer, and looked off into the distance. "Seven. This last one was eight."

As astonished as I was from the pronouncement, I wanted to learn more. I kept digging, literally and figuratively.

"Why?" I asked simply.

She let out an audible sigh. "When things went sour for me with those assholes in my squad, I knew I had to make a plan for the future. They weren't about to let me into their little gang of thieves, especially with my connection to The Bull. I gave them a hard time, threatened to make it even harder if I moved up.

"So that meant they would do whatever they had to in order to see that I didn't get the promotion. Their little empire would collapse if I was in charge. They were involved in taking down some of the biggest traffickers this state has ever seen. Do you have any idea what those drug lords will do to stay out of jail? And the ones who didn't cooperate? They'd have half of their drugs, money, and vehicles swiped by the arresting police. And we're not talking about cops on the take for nickels and dimes, or coffee and donuts here either. I mean the take was lucrative. They've got homes in Tahoe, condos in the Bahamas, exclusive golf memberships, luxury yachts. It goes on and on. You have no idea what these people have made and stashed away. So I figured, fuck it, I'd get all I could, as fast as I could."

The soil below the surface was much sandier and softer and the excavation was going quicker than expected. I was already knee deep.

I took a break and wiped my brow. "By being a hired gun?"

"I prefer contract killer," she said lightly. "It was business."

Laura saw my discomfort and it seemed to amuse her.

"I guess I'm not the sweet and innocent gal you thought I was. Not that I can help myself...." She seemed to chuckle. "You probably think I'm nuts like those guys who go out and kill because they hear voices, right? Well, sometimes I do, but they're usually a jewelry salesman or a cabana boy asking me if I need another towel." She smiled at that, brought out a pack of cigarettes, and lit one up. "I had this shrink who told me in bed once that I had some serious issues that must be dealt with, that I needed to discover the roots of my paranoia and psychosis." She shook her head sadly. "He doesn't sleep with 15-year-old patients anymore. He went to that big leather couch in the sky."

She found that funny and laughed. "I didn't even know how to spell psychopath, now I am one." She flicked her cigarette butt into my ditch. "Hurry up."

Laura looked like she was getting agitated, so I kept digging. A few minutes later I brought up something that was bothering me about all this.

"Why Mrs. Kobayashi?" I asked, striking the dirt hard. "How would you even know her?"

"I didn't," said Laura. "I met her husband when I was in Japan last year. One thing led to another and then we worked out a deal. It was all very business-like."

My shirt was soaking wet, so I took it off and tossed it on the ground. The hole was now waist deep and I was running out of time. If only I could get her closer so I could knock some sense into her head — preferably with the shovel.

"But how could you set your own uncle up?" I asked, amazed. "*Why* would you? The guy was like a father to you."

Her face clouded over. "And he was like a husband to my mother sometimes, too. I found this out when I went through her personal effects after she was gone." She lit up another smoke. "I had a hard enough time growing up with an abusive father without having to deal with that too. Hell, I don't even know for sure that it was an accident that killed my parents. They say a lot of what I have is hereditary. For all I know, my old man ran that plane into the mountain to teach my mother a lesson. It wouldn't have surprised me since my uncle was supposed to be on that flight as well. It's something I would have done, for sure."

Now a whole lot of what I wondered about Laura was becoming clearer.

"And what you were doing didn't bother you?" I asked. "Killing somebody just like that, in cold blood?"

Her face was void of expression. "I didn't feel anything, except that I was one more job closer to living the rest of my life far away from here."

I never did have very good luck with women, and Laura was par for the course. I often thought that if my life were a novel, I would be a lot like that John D. MacDonald character, Travis McGee. Far too often I fell for the sorry, "broken wing" bird and tried to nurse her back to good health, or chased the elusive dove that just wanted to be left alone — or at least not be caged by me. And seeing as McGee came out on top all the time, I longed for one of his extraordinary feats of wisdom and brilliancy that would propel me from my current predicament. But it wasn't to be. In life's game of rock, scissors, paper — gun always beats shovel.

Laura suddenly called out the last words I wanted to hear. "Okay, that's deep enough."

Chapter

Laura left me standing in my own man-made grave and opened the basket. She pulled out a shoebox and tossed it into the hole at my feet. The lid fell off and some of the contents spilled out. There were a bunch of photos of dead people with bullet holes in their foreheads, some jewelry — both men's and women's — and a lot of strange little knick-knacks.

"Those are some of my souvenirs," she said sadly. "I really wanted to keep them, but they're the only things that can tie me to what's going on."

"And there's probably some missing, right?" I countered. "Like the ones you planted on your uncle."

"You know, Jake. You've really worn out your welcome."

"Come on, Laura," I pleaded as I tried to buy some more time. "At least give the condemned man a last cigarette and a cold beer. It's the decent, humane thing to do."

My executioner stood to her full height and walked closer to the hole. "Believe me, Jake. The last thing I am is decent."

"Laura . . . please."

She raised her arm and pointed her pistol at my chest. I knew the first shots would be to take me out of commission. Once I was down, she'd finish me off with two or three to the head like all the others. There was no escape from my dilemma. I felt like a lab rat about to be put away: totally helpless.

"Goodbye, Jake."

"LAURA!"

Surprisingly, the gruff voice that shouted her name wasn't mine. She and I both turned our heads. Up on the embankment stood Lieutenant Oakley in all his six-foot-four splendor, with a long-barreled firearm of his own aimed at Laura, and a grim look pasted on his face.

"Put the gun down, Laura," he ordered. "It's over."

For the first time since I had met her, Laura Bulloch looked confused. Gone was the self-assurance, the plucky air, and the ever-present poise. In those few seconds, I watched her try to process the situation. Then, as if a switch had been thrown, her brow unfurled and she looked like she had come to a dismal conclusion.

Laura steadied her aim at me and prepared to fire.

"Don't do it, Laura!" shouted Oakley. "You shoot Morgan, I shoot you."

It was almost as if she was trying to figure out her options. If she killed me, she probably realized Oakley would have no choice but to fire. However, since I was no real threat, if she got the jump on Oakley and shot him first, she could do me at her own leisure. And if she thought about it, the lieutenant was a homicide cop who rarely had to draw his gun. She spent time at the firing range every week compared to his twice-a-year mandatory visit. I knew if I had thought of this, she had most likely, too. I could see her anxiously checking her peripheral as she worked out a plan.

In a blur, Laura dropped to one knee to reduce her vital areas and fired at Oakley. The simultaneous roar from his gun reverberated throughout the gully. My stomach sank as I saw the big cop straighten up and fall back, his firearm falling from his hand and sliding down the dirt bank toward our position.

I turned to Laura, anticipating the sound of another shot being fired and the impact of the next bullet being meant for me. As she rose to her feet, I noticed she was holding her abdomen, and a red patch of blood was seeping through her fingers. She looked down at her wound once and then at me. Shock registered on her face. Her gun hand began to turn in my direction. I grabbed the handle of the spade and threw it at her as hard as I could.

The metal business end of the shovel made a dull thud as it caromed off the side of her head. Laura was knocked to her knees with her face to the ground. I lifted myself out of the pit and started to sprint for Oakley's weapon. The crack of another shot went off and the ground near his rifle blew up into the air.

I looked over to see Laura on her haunches and trying to sight me through the blood that was running down her face. I planted my right foot and turned sharply to the left, and ran for the rim of the dune as if my life depended on it. It did.

Two more shots rang out and thudded into the earthen mound to my right. I made it to the edge of the embankment, dove, and rolled to safety. My eyes shut tight as flashes of pain exploded around my ribcage. For the moment, I knew Laura wasn't totally incapacitated and she wouldn't quit now until one of us was dead. If she finished me off, she could still fit Oakley in the same grave and get away with both of our murders. Nobody would ever find us out here. No. Laura would be relentless.

As if to substantiate my claim, I heard my name being screamed at the top of her vocal register: "JAAAAAAKKE!!!" The horrific wail sent chills down my spine. I got up and ran for the decaying train depot.

On the way, I glanced at Oakley's body, but there was no movement. I knew the keys to the Bugatti were still in my jacket in the front seat of the car, and I could go for help, but I couldn't just leave him lying out in the sand. If he wasn't already dead, Laura was determined to make sure he ended up that way. I pulled my cell phone out of the car and tried to call

911. NO SIGNAL flashed back at me. I'd have to get back to the highway to connect.

She screamed my name again.

I searched around desperately for any kind of weapon and found nothing but old pieces of timber and some nails. Then I remembered that Oakley must have driven here and most likely had some kind of back-up arsenal in his trunk. I looked around the Bugatti and 20 yards back behind the station was his unmarked green Crown Vic. I ran up to the car and tried the door. Locked. I wondered if I could get to Oakley safely and retrieve his keys and glanced in his direction to judge the distance.

"JAAAAAAKKE!!!"

The hair rose on the back of my neck as I saw a hand reach up over the edge of the embankment and claw for a hold. I frantically searched the nearby area and noticed a metal T-bar fence post leaning in the ground with a couple of strands of rusty barbwire hanging from its side.

The pole was loose and I worked it back and forth. In a few seconds it became free and I was happy to see a lump of concrete the size of a quart of paint attached to the bottom end. I raced back to the car.

There was a fourth foreboding scream.

I whipped my head around at the clarity of Laura's voice. To my dismay I spotted her at the top of the dune, on all fours as if trying to catch her breath. Oakley lay no farther than 15 feet away from her. As I was watching, I thought I saw his arm or leg move and I noticed Laura look that way.

I knew I had hardly any time. Oakley even less.

I took the metal post and drove it through the driver's window in one smash. I reached inside and opened the door and searched for the trunk release button. When the lid popped free, I ran around back. Amongst the paraphernalia and gear was a small arms case with a pistol and a box of

.38 caliber ammunition, but I didn't feel comfortable with its range. Laura was about 60 or 70 yards away and, contrary to television and the big screen, the accuracy of a sidearm would be useless. I could always throw on a Kevlar vest and charge her with the pistol, but with all that open space I'd be easy pickings. I wished Oakley had thought to put one on before going out to find us.

As hoped for, attached to the underside of the trunk lid were a Remington shotgun and a rifle. I quickly undid the fastener to the rifle and was ecstatic to find that it was a Knight's Armament SR-25, similar to the M-16. Sitting atop its rail system was a beautiful sight, literally: a Leupold 10x scope. I popped in a five-round magazine and slapped one home, then I ran around to the driver's side.

I heard two things simultaneously: one bad, one good. The first was Laura screaming at Oakley, who was up on one elbow, and the second was a distant wail of sirens announcing the cavalry had apparently arrived.

Regrettably, judging by Laura's demeanor, the lieutenant wasn't going to have the luxury of waiting for them. I wasn't sure I was even safe from her. I propped the rifle on the top of the open driver's door and flicked off the safety. Through the scope I had a clear view of an agitated Laura yelling at Oakley, who was lying prone about 10 feet away. I swung the view over to the lieutenant and saw him holding a handkerchief to a wound on the side of his neck. The cloth was crimson red. It was hard to tell which of them was bleeding out worse.

I wasn't sure what to do, whether I should wait for the backup or act now. My mind was made up for me when I saw Laura raise her gun up and aim it at Oakley.

"Please, Laura . . . don't," I pleaded in a whisper.

I had a perfect shot. I was sighted right in on her upper chest, with practically no wind and at a short range. I waited and regulated my respi-

ration as best I could. Beads of perspiration trickled down from my forehead and I pressed my skin farther into the rubber eye guard of the scope
so my sight wouldn't be hampered.

The sound of the approaching sirens must have reached Laura's ears.
With her gun still trained on Oakley, I saw her turn her head in my direction. Her face contorted in a pained expression, and then just as suddenly
relaxed.

Crack! The sound of her gun discharging resounded across the open
desert.

No! My heart sank.

I swung the scope down to Oakley. He was flat on his back, his hands
to his chest, and his eyes wide open in terror. Laura strode over and stood
above him. Without another thought, she raised her gun, pointed it at his
head, and readied herself for the kill shot.

Time had run out. I'd been holding my breath through the last
exchange and I remembered to slowly let it out. The crosshairs of my
sights were fixed steady on Laura's breastbone and I squeezed off my shot.

Boom! The .308 caliber shell impacted with her upper body so hard it
propelled her off her feet and over the edge of the embankment.

I sprinted toward Oakley as the sound of the sirens increased. I
reached his side and knelt beside him. His eyes fluttered open and shut.

"Jesus Christ . . ." he whispered hoarsely.

There was an ugly wound to the left side of the lieutenant's neck, but
the heavy flow of blood seemed to have been somewhat cauterized and
didn't look fatal. I was more concerned now with his chest as I gently
lifted his hands away.

The bullet had entered at a precise bull's-eye if you drew one on a
human torso.

Oakley tried to say something.

"Take it easy, big guy," I told him. "Help is on the way."

I crawled a few feet over and peered down the embankment. Laura lay silent in a fetal position next to the hole I had dug.

I heard the sirens stop suddenly and the sound of rubber skidding on gravel. I looked over my shoulder to see a uniform running my way.

"Call an ambulance or MEDVAC team!" I shouted. "Officer down!"

Oakley continued to try to say something.

"Save your breath," I said.

He gripped my forearm with one of his hands. With the other he slowly lifted his sweater to reveal a protective vest.

"It's like I tried to tell you, you dumb shit," he murmured. "Be prepared and always have back-up."

He was right, but still. . . . I shook my head and smiled. "You ungrateful son of a —"

More shouts and closing car doors sounded.

Oakley let go of my arm. "Okay, Hansel, give me the rifle." He began wiping down the stock and trigger. "It looks like I'm going to have to save your ass again."

Chapter

I spent all Saturday evening and the entire day Sunday as a guest of the Clark County Detention Center, and to be honest, I didn't really mind. It was a lot better than being on life support or lying on a cold slab in the morgue. Today was Monday, just after noon, and I was pulling into the parking lot of Sunrise Hospital.

I went to reception, asked for Lieutenant Oakley's room, and was given directions by a pretty nurse named Irene. As I approached the room, a figure exited.

"Morgan."

It was Alexander Bulloch, alias The Bull. I hadn't seen him since he'd been arrested and wasn't sure what his reaction would be to me after everything that had happened. Including the exposure and death of his niece, Laura.

He came over and shook my hand. "I appreciate everything you did to get me out of the mess I was in, and I'm sorry for what you had to go through."

I just nodded as there wasn't much I could, or wanted to, say.

"I loved Laura like a daughter," he said softly. "I don't know where things went wrong, but you know . . . at times I think I would trade places with her if it would mean she could continue her life without the demons that were within her . . . somehow spare her from the pain and despair she must have been suffering."

He shook his head, and although it was accompanied by a small chuckle, his eyes were moist. "You know, Morgan, I haven't been to church in over 20 years. But I'm going to go over to St. Christopher's in a little while and say a couple of prayers: one for thankfulness, and one for forgiveness on sweet Laura's soul."

The man was bordering on sainthood, as far as I was concerned, for feeling that way after how she had set him up.

"And you're still going through with your retirement, I take it?"

"Eventually," he said. "We found a ton of paperwork, photos, and video at Laura's house. All of it pertaining to how she was going to take down the bad eggs in her squad. I'm not in any big hurry now, really. I think I'm going to take care of this last bit of garbage, then I'll have plenty of time to play golf."

I smiled back at him. "You do that, Bull."

"Only my friends call me Bull," he informed me.

I just looked back at him, startled.

"And I consider you one of them."

He patted me on the shoulder and walked slowly down the hall.

"Hey, good-lookin'," I called out as I entered the room.

You could tell his family and friends had already visited by all the cards and flowers that were spread about. A big string of cut-out letters hanging across the window spelled out *Get well soon, Dad!*

Oakley was lying in bed, propped up reading a copy of *Police Chief.*

"Gee, pretty heady stuff," I said, pointing to the magazine. "But you'll have to be able to shoot a firearm a lot better if you want to make chief."

The lieutenant scowled back at me and put the issue under his pillow with the rest of his dreams. Then he pointed to his neck, shook his head, and made a quack-quack motion with his hand.

Luckily, I could read basic, child's sign language.

"Ah," I said. "You can't talk."

He made a sewing motion with his finger and thumb.

"Stitches."

He nodded.

"You're allowed to eat, right?"

Apparently he didn't know how to sign the word "soft," so he wrote it on a pad he kept at his side.

"Well, have I got a surprise for you," I said as I opened the bag I had brought. I took out an extra large black coffee and a dozen Krispy Kreme donuts.

Oakley's eyes went wide. He reached out both arms toward me and made puckering noises with his lips.

"You can kiss me later," I told him. "Eat first."

He grabbed a plastic bowl of Jell-O and a Styrofoam cup of water from the rolling bedside table and tossed them in the nearby wastebasket. Then he stuck a thick straw in the coffee and opened the box of goodies. He took a bite, smiled, and gave me a big thumb's up, then he pointed to a chair for me to sit.

"So I spent the last two days in Detention," I told him.

Oakley raised an eyebrow.

"It wasn't so bad. I told them exactly what you told me to tell them. I busted into your car and brought you the rifle. You did all the shooting. I was just an innocent bystander who got caught in the crossfire. Nothing more. Nothing less. And just like you said, they didn't run roughhouse over me. They didn't exactly take me in with warm hugs, but it could've been a lot worse."

He licked some icing off his fingers and drew two letters in the air.

"Yup, you're right. They just had to cross their T's and dot their I's. I think it was more of a 'satisfying the paperwork' project if you ask me. I got the feeling that even if what I was telling them wasn't exactly the way things went down, they didn't mind as long as it matched up with what you reported. I just felt they really didn't want any kind of publicity on this one. And who can blame them, all things considered. Come to think of it, I've never seen anything hushed up this tight since I got tossed from the force. There was a lot to cover up there, too."

Oakley went for another glazed treat. He suddenly seemed to remember something and snapped his fingers. I watched as he unbuttoned his pajama shirt and pointed to an ugly purple bruise where the Kevlar vest had stopped the .38 caliber.

"Looks nasty," I said. "And there I was worried that you hadn't thought to put one on. Which reminds me, I'm glad you picked up on The Dead Man's Hand I tossed out the window, or I would've been one."

He tapped his finger to his temple and I smiled along with him.

"So I guess The Bull updated you on what's going down with Vice?"

The lieutenant nodded, then jotted something on the pad. He held it up for me: *Serves the bastards right!*

"Yeah, I'm pretty sure that I'll be the last person on Theodore Parker and his boys' minds. They're going to be a little preoccupied to pay me any attention."

I watched Oakley munching away.

"I hope you realize all this was a result of you wanting to have a body cavity search done on me for a casino chip?"

He smiled sheepishly.

"I owe you one," I told him, getting up from the chair.

The lieutenant took one more donut from the box and hid the rest in a drawer of his nightstand. He put his index finger vertically in front of his mouth. "Ssshh."

I stood beside him. "How much longer they going to keep you in here?"

He shrugged his burly shoulders and held up one finger and then two.

"Two or three days?"

Oakley nodded.

"I think you'll probably have a couple of weeks off work coming to you," I said. "Are you planning on just hanging around the house?"

He shook his head adamantly and pretended he was dealing out cards.

I couldn't help but chuckle. "Be careful, you big fish."

Oakley wrote on the pad: *Thanks for saving my life, Jake.* Then he pointed up to the get well sign his kids had made for him.

I reached out my hand and he took it in his big paw.

"And I thank you for saving mine. . . ." I left that phrase hanging there for a second but held his grip. "You know, I've known you for over a year and three murder cases now, and I've never learned your first name."

He let go of my hand and wrote: *Some cop you were!*

I grinned as he continued writing. When he finished he held it up for me: *Here's a clue — my parents were huge Beatles fans. . . . Okay? Are you happy now?*

I smiled more and nodded.

Good. Now get lost. My sleepy time is coming up.

I laughed and said, "Don't forget to wipe the crumbs off your bed." Then I walked to the doorway, where I turned and shot him with my finger.

"See ya, *Ringo!*"

I managed to duck into the hallway before the pen he threw hit me.

I sat in the parking lot for a few minutes and I decided to make one unscheduled stop.

♦

I hadn't been one of the faithful flock since Karen's funeral almost four years ago, but St. Christopher's welcomed me all the same. The church was vacant except for one lone figure in the third front row. I made my way up the aisle and slid into the pew beside The Bull. He glanced over as if he knew it might be me, pursed his lips, and continued with his thoughts. I knelt there quietly with thoughts of my own: the first were for Karen and for what she had meant; the next were intended solely for me to remind myself of the path I had chosen; the last was for Laura, to forgive what she had become. I quietly left Alexander Bulloch alone without interrupting his prayers.

♥

The next stop I made took the better part of two hours.

♠

The last one found me driving down Meadow Brook Lane for the second time in a week. The only difference this time was that I hadn't called ahead of time. I pulled into the driveway, circumvented the same collection of kid's toys, and rang the doorbell.

The lady of the house came to the door and recognized me right away.

"Jake Morgan," she said with surprise, obviously not sure why I would be there.

"Hello, Helena," I replied. "I come bearing gifts."

Her surprise slowly evolved into mild shock and a beautiful wide smile came to her face. "Whatever are you talking about?" she asked in her wonderful Russian accent.

Her two children came charging down the hall and stopped at the doorway to see who was there. A moment later the little white terrier skidded to a stop at the threshold, bared his bottom row of teeth again, and reminded me who the protector of the family was.

"Well, first of all, I'm returning the Tupperware you loaned me for that delicious borscht." I handed the plastic container to her. "I even remembered to clean it first," I told her proudly.

She grinned and held back a laugh.

"Next," I announced brightly to the children as I handed them a colorful plastic bag.

Both of them looked up to their mother first. When Helena smiled and nodded her head, the kids emptied the bag.

"*Narnia! Narnia!*" shouted the little girl while her brother yelled over her, "*Shrek! Shrek!*" The two of them took off back down the hallway while the terrier tried to get traction to follow.

Helena snickered into her hand. "That was very thoughtful of you."

"And last, but not least," I said with just a touch of suspense as I handed her the green tin box. "Cookies!"

Her eyes went wide as she began to laugh. "A *Santa* cookie container? In *June?*"

"It's just a little something I dug up," I said dismissively. "For you and your hard-working police benevolent group."

"Thank you. I will bring it to our meeting tonight," she said with a smile that could have lit up The Strip. "You are certainly full of surprises, Jake Morgan."

"You could say that again," I agreed as I reminded myself of what was inside. And because of doing this for Karen's memory, I had resisted the temptation of taking more than a dozen 'cookies' for my next poker stake. In a weird way, Karen would have understood. "Sometimes I even surprise myself."

"Well, why don't you come inside, Jake?" Helena said. "I've got some cabbage rolls just about ready to come out of the oven."

"Mmm," I said as I sniffed the air. "I thought I smelled something scrumptious."

Helena glanced down as she was about to let me in.

"Oh, my God, Jake," she said, shaking her head but still smiling. "Look at you."

I peered down to see my cuffs and shoes covered in a light coating of dirt.

"Oops, sorry," I apologized sheepishly as I took a broom from the porch and swept my legs and feet.

"It looks as if you were playing in a sand lot," Helena stated.

"I was," I told her as I replaced the broom and followed her toward the kitchen. "A really, really big one."